CRIMSON

BEN WISE

www.ben-wise.com

Cover art by
www.SelfPubBookCovers.com/Daniela

ISBN: 0994194722
ISBN-13: 978-0-9941947-2-5

This is a work of fiction. Names, characters, businesses,
places, events and incidents either are the products of
the author's imagination or used in a fictitious manner.
Any resemblance to actual persons, living or dead, or
actual events is purely coincidental.

ACKNOWLEDGMENTS

Firstly, thanks to Schwartzie, a black kitty first and a willing friend second, who puts up with me far too much on Facebook and many other mediums while I toiled away and was still willing to offer story and editing advice (but no thanks for insisting I rename Chelsea). More than just an editor, she has been a wonderful mentor and amazing wall upon which to throw my ideas. To my other test readers, Cornell and Kaden, who suffered through the unedited manuscript despite it making no sense whatsoever and were still willing to politely lie and say they enjoyed it and offer advice along the way. To Allison, for allowing me to use her namesake and image, more beautiful than the character could ever be. And finally to Erin, the reader of my final draft, who gave me the best feedback a new author could ever have gotten by reading the whole thing within the day and who's first response was to ask excitedly for the next book.

Red Night

Per usual, tonight is another fucking long night. The rain has eased; the wet keeping most of the usual menagerie away. A line of crows huddle in black silhouette on a roof across the street as they suffer their watery fate together in the cold drizzle. Below them, a couple of traders are sticking it out, selling their chosen products; nothing of value. A few food stalls remain open, the ones that never close no matter the weather. But even they seem quiet tonight. The usual gang of younger abandoneds are making the usual nuisance of themselves and of course tonight's scene wouldn't be complete without the usual old guy acting in his usual creepy way sitting on his usual bench at the stall he never seems to leave. I'm fairly certain I've never actually seen him move from it.

Aine and I lean against the dirty red brick wall of our usual haunt - an empty alley corner within sight of anything worth seeing on the main road that acted as the focal point for our broken little community. Rain pours onto the street from a tin roof above us; the water pooling around a mess of debris filling the street, the

1

remains of a society not long lost. The suburb still wears the aftermath of the war, like it ended yesterday. Even after twenty years. I figure most of us have simply tuned out the debris. To me it's just part of the landscape.

But as children growing up, it meant there was always something to explore. Always things to scavenge. And these days it's home, comfort in its lack thereof. I haven't ever really felt any desire to travel beyond this place. Perhaps one day I'll visit other abandoned suburbs, but now? I can never manage to justify the effort to myself. What's difference is there between one broken suburb and another? I won't pretend like it's always been easy to live here. Perhaps it's comfort in the familiar?

Of course, the inner city is out of the question. I hear about the people who live there, all crammed together in high-rises and apartments. It must be stifling to live so close to one another like that. Here, there are enough derelict buildings that we could each have one to live in if we wanted. But even if I did consider trying to survive in the inner city, how long would it be before I was detected? Why risk it? There's nothing there for me.

There mustn't be enough of us out here for the government to see us as a problem. The inner city dwellers consider the suburbs across the Virdis River abandoned. The provisional law enforcement doesn't bother with us. On purpose, I suspect. Too much work. Sure they know we exist but nobody cares about us anymore. I guess they'd rather pretend we didn't exist. It could have turned out worse for me. We don't cross the river into the inner suburbs where all the non-talented flocked during the war and they don't cross it to come out here. Not that the government would let them. Still, it doesn't hurt to avoid drawing attention to ourselves, despite the fact that it's been a long time since individuals of our nature have been an issue.

Aine had been pouring out her thoughts to me all afternoon, a stream of desire, boredom and the paranoia people of our position in society have. I had given up even nodding and pretending to listen a good 15 minutes ago. She has such a short attention span that I'm not sure she's even noticed. Maybe she's just looking for someone to pay attention to her. It's a common theme among us abandoneds. We're all looking for somebody to pay attention to us, one way or another. Even in this community, and that word must get used lightly, we are all ultimately on our own. The younger kids show their lack of parental figures, but by our age, we've mostly gone past that. For us, it's all about companionship.

So I can't really blame her. She does get a lot more attention than I do. And it's always complicated with her. My love life, on the other hand, is pretty simple. It doesn't exist. Most girls, like Aine, are lucky with the fact that a lot more boys than girls were abandoned when we were children. Things have turned out less favourably for me. There are few girls around here that share my romantic interests. None, in fact. And it's not like there's a lot of new girls coming into the community that might change the balance up. So, I end up spending a lot of time by myself. But I enjoy being with Aine regardless, I enjoy her company.

It's strange how we ended up friends. I guess we just gravitated towards each other since we could scrape together some small bit of commonality with our close ages. There really aren't many other girls around here. We don't really have much in common beyond age and we certainly don't think alike. But she is a good person; beautiful in her own way. We get along.

Like everybody in this community of outcasts, we had all tested positive for talent and been abandoned early in our childhood. By parents who just couldn't bring it upon themselves to hand over their children to the government and 'do the right thing' for society. Talented, hah, once upon a time it used to be a positive word. With the fall of the talented government and its subsequent destruction, now it's just a stigma attached to those of us unlucky enough to be born this way.

At least Aine knows her switch; I can't say the same for me. Around the age of five every child is tested for the potential to develop talents, not that I remember anything back that far. It's a series of tests, where each test measures a child for an affinity to a particular type of talent, called a birth switch. I couldn't tell you what happens in them though; frankly I don't remember anything before being here, on the streets of this abandoned suburb. Around 9 percent of children test positive and as far as I know, nobody has been found to have more than one switch. It's genetic in some way but I can never remember the details. The switch you're born with is the anchor around your neck for the rest of your life. At least, that's how Aine sees it.

I don't know though. Most kids start showing basic signs of their switch when they start growing up. Then there's puberty, which really sends a kid's talent crazy; it was hard to miss that stage with Aine, which often involved dodging objects she randomly flung around the place according to her mood.

Aine's a kine, a minor telekinetic. She can move light objects, maybe push a chair around and stuff, the usual shit, nothing special. These days, since the war and the government's weeding out of talented children before they grow up, it's rare for anybody to develop more than that. Sure, there are a few who manage beyond that, but nothing like they say the talented had during the war. Even the most talented paths and clairs are a shadow of their former selves. By around sixteen or so, almost everyone's talent is fully developed.

In my case though all I had developed by sixteen was sufficient to attract the attention of boys who grew up here. Most got the hint pretty quickly. Thankfully Aine quickly caught up and now diverts most of the attention away from me. Sometimes, a little more physically convincing has been required. Such is life in this community. I deal.

Since the events of the veil war and the fall of the talented governance, parents have been required to hand over any talented children for schooling. Schooling is for the greater good of society to prevent another veil war they say. They avoid mentioning, of course, that no child has ever been returned from schooling. Nobody knows what happens to them, though I could give it a pretty good guess. Most parents are 'convinced', forcibly or by fear, by the new government to do the right thing by society and prevent the possibility of talents ever being in control of things ever again. They like to use phrases like 'It's the right thing for your child' and 'Do the right thing by society'. I wonder if there is anybody who believes the government. I wonder if the government cares.

Still, there are always a few parents that just can't bring themselves to hand their children over and choose instead abandon them to the streets. If they don't start out in the abandoned suburbs those who survive end up there. Or one of the other abandoned suburbs dotted around the outer city. Question: is being abandoned by your parents and left to fend for yourself really a better life? Hah, such a melancholic thought. Aine isn't the only one looking for attention. It isn't so bad, I promise. I've survived.

Did I mention today was boring as fuck? Emphasis on was. That creepy old guy across the street just stood up, looked across at us and started yelling. That's the first time I think I've ever heard a word from the guy. Shit, it's probably the first time I've ever seen him move. This is a guy old enough to have experienced the war. My mind catches this thought and runs with it for a moment. It probably should have been listening to what he's yelling instead.

"Run!"

The message finally starts to sink in, forcing its way into my head. It still takes a moment for me to comprehend why he's gesturing wildly. It's then I notice Aine tugging on my arm. It slipped my attention, just like the police rushing towards us.

"Shit."

I think that's the first word I've spoken today. We bolt down the alley, for what little good it does us. We make three steps when Aine slips on the wet pavement. Shit. I reach back to pull her up. My fingers brush against her arm before a hand pushes me away. My captor shoves me back against the red brick. Aine is thrown beside me. I see her squirm against a hand pressed against her chest.

Time seems to flowing wrong. Perhaps it's the adrenaline. I don't know why I don't struggle, as if I'm not supposed to. I feel disconnected from reality. This feels wrong. This is all so very, very wrong. But I can't corral my thoughts into anything meaningful. All I'm able to focus on is how distinct her blonde hair stands out from the deep red brick. How messy it looks caught against the abrasive wall. She is normally so fastidious about it.

Beyond the cop holding me, there's an older woman; her unfamiliar ash coloured uniform implies her importance, paramilitary perhaps. She wears it far too well to be local police. It's unadorned by anything identifiable except for a pristine white band that wraps around her upper arm. Why would one of them come all the way out here to this place? That question goes unanswered when I notice the young woman standing quietly beside her. Her attractiveness is lost in the utilitarianism of her navy outfit. Definitely not a cop.

She stands diminutively next to the soldier, under her control perhaps? She massages her wrist, almost subconsciously. Then it strikes me, she's talented. I flash a confused look at her, but her eyes just look blankly past me. Then I see her forehead form into a knot of confusion. She's pretty, her dark hair falling over striking green eyes. What's her purpose here?

"Well?" the woman asks impatiently.

"The blonde's telekinetic," the girl responds timidly.

"And this dark haired one?" the cop holding me interjects.

Our eyes meet. My mind latches onto the brilliant green of her irises, as if it's suddenly the only thing that matters right now. It's been so long since I've seen a face like it. Not since... and then the thought is lost. She hesitates, her eyes casting about as if she hopes to avoid answering the question I didn't know to ask.

"I don't know," she eventually replies.

The police turn their heads as one to stare at her.

"You don't know?" both the soldier and the cop holding me ask in unison.

"I don't know," she stammers, "she's talented, no doubt. She doesn't read like any typical switch. It's so subtle it's barely noticeable. And there's nobody shielding her either, it's just..." The girl's voice drops as the sentence trails off, head shaking. "Look," she continues, "she's definitely piercing the veil which confirms her as talented. But..."

"You know exactly what she is, don't you?" the woman asks.

She just nods, as if ashamed.

"What do you want to do?" the cop holding me asks the older woman.

She nods to herself. "Bring her in."

I pick up on how 'her' was emphasised.

Bring me where? Blink. The cop holding Aine presses something against her head. Blink. Aine is falling to the ground, the gun a black shadow over her. Blink. I look down but can't seem to work out why she's fallen. Time isn't flowing right again. Somewhere in the back of my head, a voice recites a piece of rote knowledge learnt long ago; not even the most talented of telekinetics can affect the course of a bullet. Why this is important? I blink. Deep red paints Aine's blonde hair away; it slowly surrenders to the wall behind her.

The cop holding me swings the butt of his gun against my head. Time stops flowing completely and I can only embrace the incoming darkness.

Shattered Glass

I wake up on a hard cot surrounded by the white walls of a tiny room. At least they used to be white; it's been a while since they could be called white. I can't tell if this is some nightmarish hospital room or a foul clinical prison. The fluorescent fails the room. It couldn't get more like something out of a ghastly nightmare.

Stabbing pain hits me in the face, right where the pistol connected with my cheek. It's not enough to stop me passing out again.

◆

Noise. The walls are still white. Face still hurts. I'm completely naked; when did that happen? Noise. Somebody fumbling with a door. Door? As the door opens the light in the room flares intensely white, blinding me; two dark shapes against the searing light enter the room. My eyes focus as the first shape grabs me roughly by the arm and pulls me to my feet.

My sight begins to recover. The shape's ash uniform comes into focus, aligning his allegiance with the woman at my capture. The sub machine gun strapped to his body is nothing like the handguns the local police carry. But what scares me is the half metre long scabbard that hangs by his thigh and the long knife that surely fits inside it.

The look he flashes me can only be described as wicked. His fist follows, connecting with my stomach. It doubles me over, but that isn't what really hits me. Aine's death finally registers. The memory of previous events come rushing back into my head. The weight of it all drops me to my knees. The guard grabs me roughly, his hands groping over me. Never seen a naked girl before? Whatever.

He lifts me by my armpits and pulls me out of the room. Heels dragging, I just let it happen. It's a chance to take the place in. Dragged into a hallway, long and more not-white; twisted hospital indeed. The walls of this hallway have more of a green tinge than the brown of the room where I woke. There are more doors down from what was mine but our destination is just one door down, the room at the end of the hallway.

The guard throws me down near the centre of the room. A single lamp suspended from the middle of the ceiling, highlights the old hospital gurney that waits underneath but fails to breach the shadows of the corners of the room. Rusty steel rails frame the gurney, leather straps hang from each side. The nightmare gets worse.

If it wasn't for the two guards standing stiffly at the door cradling sub machine guns and the fact that the room looks not to have been cleaned in 50 years, it'd almost seem like this was a surgery.

"Get on the bed," the accompanying guard snaps at me.

The two guards react instantly to a returned blank stare, coming alive in sync and pointing their guns at me with obvious intent. They start to circle around me hesitantly, as if I am some wounded animal about to lash out. Can't imagine what they think I could be capable of in the shape I'm in at the moment. Delightful; it would appear I'm not here for a general check-up. It would seem though, that arguing the point is probably not in my best interest.

Their continued stares flick a switch in my head and I start to become a lot more self-conscious. Normally I wouldn't give a shit; privacy isn't something one expects much of on the streets. And I've dealt with similar stares before but not with men of their stature.

I pull myself onto the bed. The mattress is hard foam, less a bed than a padded mat. My captor guard shoves me back impatiently, holding me down roughly with one hand while one of the door guards steps forward to fasten the leather straps over my wrists. Far too tight. Lying back as I am, the pain in my head quickly comes back to me and with it memories of Aine. Damn.

On the upper arm of the guard holding me down is a white band stained with a red cross. I've seen that before. I remember, when I was captured the woman's uniform had the same band. All the guards in the room are wearing one. I don't recognise its meaning.

"Do we bind her?" the guard appears to ask nobody.

"For the moment I don't think that's necessary. Let's see what happens, no?" a voice from the corner replies.

Where the fuck did she come from? The older woman, the soldier from before materialises out of the dark and stands over me.

"Hello little one," she starts. "You are an honoured guest of the Poor Fellow-Soldiers of Christ and of the Temple of Solomon. The Order of the Temple – The Knights Templar if you will. We've obviously met before, but I apologise for not introducing myself earlier. You, little one, you may call me Levia."

The Templars? Shit, really? The Templars have a vicious reputation for being at the forefront of persecution. Most people born post war believe them to be a myth, a scary tale told to keep children in line. Until today, I believed they were a myth as well. Their supposed methods are the subject of many rumours, none pleasant.

"You have to understand," she continues in a manner that's far too matter of fact, "that we have, kept almost complete control of the development of talent in the wild for some time now. Yes, even keeping a watch on those who live in the outer suburbs. We made sure that there will be noone capable of developing their talent to the extent of the traitors to humanity during the war. And yet, here you are; something else entirely. And given how we found you, it begs the question; if you are what we think you are, how did you avoid us for so long? We wiped out your kind. So we need to find out, are you what we think you are? If there's even a small chance... well we can't risk humanity to have somebody with such a twisted nature running around. You understand I hope?" Her face screws up in mock seriousness. "So, you could save us all a lot of heartache and just tell us."

I give her my best attempt at a serious look back. "I have no idea."

"That's ok. I understand you wouldn't have had anybody to teach you. It'll be more fun this way. We'll find out. The next stage is to run some, well, one might call them more advanced tests than the typical ones you'd find out there," she motions to imply the world outside, "but we've found them to be pretty reliable, really. If you push anyone hard enough, eventually the body's own fight or flight response will kick in and, for a talented person that means instinctually attempting whatever their talent allows them. For you, I expect that might be quite spectacular. It will certainly be interesting to see how you connect with the veil.

"Or, we push too hard," she shrugs and smiles down at me, "then it stops being an issue. But don't fear, it shouldn't take too long and Eli is very good at what he does. We'll work you out."

I hear the door to the room open and slow, heavy footsteps approach.

"This is Eli. He'll be carrying out the testing," Levia says.

Eli follows, "Thankfully, we were able to put many of the tools your kind abandoned after the war, so we can carry out these tests. And while you might wonder

14

how we Templars reconcile the use of the twisted tools of our enemy, in circumstances like these we must be pragmatic. We could never develop such twisted tools ourselves you see. Besides, they're welcome to join us here and ask for them back if they want them returned," he laughs.

He holds a section of thin copper piping above me, roughly a foot long. Down its length, copper wire is woven in a pattern over two-thirds of the pipe. The wire seems to be wound in a single direction, as if the entire pattern's shapes point toward one end. The light in the room plays across the wiry pattern, dark shadows suggesting sinister things. He holds the wire-free end of the pipe, which I guess is the handle of whatever it is.

"The pattern maintains a construct designed to amplify suggestive elements from the sender into the mind of the receiver. The device focuses and directs that programming. It is, to give your kind some credit, an interesting telepathic device."

He smiles as he touches the device to the inside of my wrist. I scream as searing pain shoots through every nerve in my arm. As he drags the device up, I can feel the bones in my arm shattering while the flesh around them tears off. He lifts the device off when he reaches the inside of my elbow. I've run out of air to keep screaming. Breathe. Down at my arm I expect to see nothing but bloody gore, but to my confusion there's no noticeable effect at all. What the fuck is happening?

He responds to my confusion, twisted visibly on my face. "The device is only suggestive; it merely suggests the pain I think of. Your mind is kind enough to fills in the rest. We couldn't in good conscience, as keepers of the faith, actually damage a person in our care, even a heathen like you, now could we?"

The rhetorical question is lost on me.

"It would be against our nature, quite unlike the savages of your kind, the ones who would develop such a thing in the first place."

The device presses into my shoulder; my body twists and thrashes in a vain attempt to escape the searing pain. In my struggle my leg kicks out toward him. Not that I can control doing it. There's nothing but blinding pain.

He flashes me an angry look and turns to the guards. "Going to have to strap this fiend in, hold her legs apart damn it."

Each guard roughly grabs a leg as I struggle but they're far too strong for me to help myself. Thick leather straps tighten around my ankles, left first then right. I'm left spread-eagled and exposed, too shocked to make my voice work, too shocked to say anything at all.

He drives the copper wand hard into the bones of my pelvis. The light dims and the room floods with darkness. Or is that just my mind blacking out? I can't think straight enough to tell the difference. In the distance somebody is screaming. Me. My pelvis shatters like glass into a million pieces. The light bulb above me shatters and glass dust covers me like a mist. It's almost beautiful.

The pain stops. I open my eyes to the room still in darkness.

"A response, good," Levia says from over in the corner again. "That will do for the moment. Put her out and fix this damn light"

I don't notice the needle. Everything goes dark again.

♦

Light. Curled up, I'm back in the bed of the first room. Still naked, the glass dust cleaned off me. Not sure I want to know how this occurred. No, not completely naked – around my wrists are copper coloured bracelets, an inch or so wide. No, not copper coloured, they actually are copper. The light plays off the metal, the surface visibly perfect. And they won't come off. I can't see any join, but they're too small to slide over my hands. The cold feeling of the copper against my wrists brings back the events last experienced. Panic sets in. What's their purpose?

Levia's voice from the corner of the room answers my unasked question, "Another device we acquired. The bracelets act a valve for the flow of energy. When placed on someone who is talented they prevent them from using their ability but ensure that the link isn't completely broken between the talent and the veil. That's important, obviously, we can't just cut the link but we need to keep your mind under control to prevent further mishaps, don't we?

"Now, yesterday was just the introduction, today we should get to see what makes you tick." I see the wicked smile on her face as she marches out of the room.

Guards pass her as she leaves; they drag me back to the other room. I'm too afraid now to resist.

The light is brighter this time and yet somehow the room seems so much darker. The cast shadows dance wickedly around the room. Screams quickly fill the room. If only time could flow a little faster. I don't remember it ending.

Again and again I wake up to this. Sometimes I don't even realise I've woken up before the session ends. Who can tell the difference between one nightmare and another? This was the better life you wanted your daughter to live?

Worse, they are becoming more frustrated. Things aren't going to plan. I'm not working as expected. The door opens again. By now, the guards have given up all pretence of avoiding harm to me. The fist to my face establishes their frustration and drops me to my knees. Looking down in the daze I notice that the room isn't completely white. Confusion reigns. Somebody is yelling. Vivid drops of crimson rebel against the white concrete floor. My rebellion. I fall face first.

A Dark Lesson

Again I find myself crucified on their hospital rack. My lips taste metallic; blood still flows down my face. The room feels colder, distinctly more sinister, if that were even possible. The guards at the door are stiffer, holding their guns tighter. The tension in the room is distinct. Where's Levia?

"Shall we find out what you are today?" Eli's voice has a new edge to it, cold and harsh.

Today there's no flourish with the device, no false politeness in his voice. I meet his stare. Today the device starts between my thighs. It was almost like I had grown used to the pain of previous sessions. Not today. I don't know where I find the breath to scream. The device seems to respond to Eli's sadistic nature even more so today. It pushes painfully against my skin as he drags it up my pelvis. By the time it reaches my stomach I've lost control, thrashing wildly. Blood dripping down my throat adds the fear of drowning. Panic sets in as he pulls the device off just before my chest. He'd always avoided my chest thus far.

Eli leans over me. "I want you to scream for me."

His face twists into pure malevolence and shoves the wand between my breasts. My ribs implode inwards, piercing my lungs in a thousand places. My body arches as my spine fuses into a twisted bridge of bone. Fiery heat spreads across my chest. One final beat of my heart thumps in my ears before it explodes. Time stops.

♦

Despite the glow of the light above me, the room is inexplicitly dark. And yet, the darkness comes with its own comforting warmth. The room remains frozen, the people surrounding me motionless.

Out of darkness a shadowy figure steps towards me. The figure, feminine and graceful, is an empty void of black in the now inadequate darkness of the room. Featureless but for the deep red glow of her eyes, her exact shape is hidden in a soft smoky fog, as black as the figure herself.

A quiet and gentle voice, a familiar tone softly says, "You don't have to go through this anymore. We can leave. These people can't keep you here."

Her hand reaches out and strokes my cheek. I can't feel it at first. As she runs her hand carefully down my arm I almost feel her become more corporal. The feeling is there for just a fleeting moment before it's gone again. The leather straps holding me down fall apart. She beckons me upright and laughs gently. Her hands touch the bracelets on my wrists.

"These are just toys to please fools like these. They only suggest control while your mind does the actually work filling in the blanks. They can't truly control you and they definitely can't really stop you using your talents. You'll understand, one day. I promise."

Her hand touches the side of my head and I start to see black energy leak as lines of weakness form across the bracelets. They split from my wrists, yet defy gravity as they remain hovering in place. All the raw energy in the room floods back into me, shocking in its suddenness.

She says gently, "This lesson can't last forever though. Fate doesn't like it when you try to mess with time too much. Let me teach a little of what it means to be you as we get you out of here. The rest you'll have to learn for yourself. I'm sure you'll be fine.

"You are not like the other talented, you were never meant to be locked into a single talent; you're a totally blank canvas. During the first war there was more of our type, a lot more, but, well, the veil war happened. The actual veil war, not the sadistic orgy of violence these immoral bastards started after.

"Those born with a set talent use energy differently, when they drag it through the veil, it converts to a refined form, something a little more suited to this side of the veil. They don't even realise they're doing it. The way that it is refined seems to have a lot to do with what talent comes naturally to a born talented. In direct and fair competition, they'll be better than you ten out of ten times given the same level of experience and energy. But you, you were born free from those restraints. You can pierce through the veil and access the raw material.

You're free to manipulate it however your mind is capable.

"Let me give you a taste," she says, her eyes glowing redder.

"First, telepathy and with it mind control." A stream of black energy follows her hand as she pulls it away from my head. She walks over and joins the stream with the head of one of the frozen door guards with a gentle caress.

"You form an image in your mind of the actions you want the person to commit to, then push the suggestion across a connection with the other person. Minds are amazingly capable of filling in the little details if you give them just the slightest nudge."

Her head tilts and an image forms in my head - each door guard lift their gun up and take aim at the other.

"Second, telekinesis or psychokinesis, whichever you fancy." Her hand passes over my head again and two black tendrils snake out. She manipulates the energy deftly, wrapping it around the handles of the knives the guards carry on their belts.

"Telekinesis requires a certain physical shift in thinking that can only be felt rather than thought. This shift requires a lot more energy input than telepathy to achieve a useful result, but still, you'll work it out."

And I do feel it as each knife is lifted from their sheaths. I guess I could only describe it as if the energy connections feel like they're another limb.

"Yes, it's really is like that, like another limb," she says.

Each highly polished knife is more than a foot in length, shit, almost long enough to be a sword. Each reminds me of a beak, a single straight edge while the spine curves down to the point at the tip. The knives float towards the last guard, hovering point first over each depression formed by the clavicles at his neck.

"Third lesson and most important, Constructs. Constructs are a unique talent, certainly among the born talented. When most talented use their ability, how it happens, the details, are all automatic. Their mind subconsciously works out the necessary details but they really have little control over it. Constructs, on the other hand, are energy based devices designed, programmed is the right term, by the user to achieve a certain task. Constructs, on the other hand, are energy based devices designed, programmed is the right term, by the creator to achieve a certain task. You take a bunch of raw energy, form it into an appropriate shape then plan out how you want it to act. You can make it take on any ability you know, assuming you pump enough energy into it to keep it going. They are energy machines. You're truly limited only by how much you can keep in your imagination. Don't forget that. The connections you're forming now with these people are, in their own way, the most basic of constructs. The device Eli used on you is a construct as well. It's been associated with a physical object to allow anybody to use it, but it's still a construct. Now that you have access to it you can manipulate it freely. Let's tweak it a little."

Her eyes glow red again. The device floats across the room, the patterned end pushing into the throat of Eli.

"Time's almost up. Last lesson, clairvoyance."

An image flashes into my head. I can see the old man sitting across from me. The thought comes and goes quickly, like a memory, but it's not one I've ever had.

"He's avoided talking to you long enough."

"And that's all I can teach you for now. You'll find the rest out. Trust. You have some trying times ahead, but also some beautiful ones as well. You have some hard decisions to make, but I know you do fine."

She leans over and kisses me on the forehead. Then she's gone. Time comes rushing back and light defeats dark once again. Once white turns red.

Eli's head simply explodes. Red mist fills the room; his body collapsing as life slowly pours from his neck and pools around his fallen body. The knives slide through the neck of the first guard then shear sideways through his neck. Blood fountains from his carotid arteries. Twin guards standing in mirror image unload their weapons on full automatic. Two walls red in reflected repercussion.

Two copper bracelets clatter on the floor. It's over in a moment. Bloody hell.

The floor is slick with blood as I step through the destruction. The impact of what just occurred slows my footsteps, guards slumped at the door are stepped over nervously. Watchfully I open the door to stumble into the dark hallway. An open hall cupboard further down is stacked with old hospital gowns. I take one to cover myself with. Heavy footsteps filter down from a staircase at the end of the hallway. The door nearest provides a quick hiding place. Breathe. Boots pound pass the door.

"Find her!" Levia's voice shouts down the hall.

Seems to me like a pretty good time to not be here anymore. I make a dash for the staircase. Levia and those with her react instantly. A sign on the wall tells me that I'm below ground. The volume of boots hitting vinyl increases but I'm far too scared to turn around and look back at my pursuers.

"Don't shoot her!" Levia yells down the hallway.

I duck my head and launch myself into the concrete stairwell. Boots hit concrete just as I turn the first corner of the stairs. I don't make it one flight up. An arm grabs me and I go no further.

"I've got her," An unfamiliar guard says.

I struggle in his grip. Think. Remember what happened in the room before. How do I make this shit work? More footsteps reverberate up the stairwell.

"Hold her!" Levia shouts up the staircase.

This is not working; time for Plan B. What's Plan B? I don't know either. I twist in the guard's grip trying to break free. It's too tight, this isn't working either.

There. I reach out. The knife from his belt slips out easily. He's quick to drop me after I start swinging wildly. Don't know if I hit him or not but now's not the time to find out. Too close. Up two flights of stairs; ground floor, shoulder first through the stairwell doors. The lobby is a blur. Shoulder first through the swinging glass doors. That was definitely a mistake. The doors are much heavier than expected. I stumble outside, the afternoon sun blinding.

"Here, quickly, into the car!" yells a man.

He stands next to a dark sedan sitting a few strides from the front door; dark tinted windows with engine running. It's not like I could change directions anyway. A back door is already open. The stranger grabs me as I get near the vehicle and pushes me rather ungracefully into the waiting car. Doors slam shut, tyres squeal. What the fuck just happened? Who are these people? I panic.

Resist

"Do I want to know who the hell you are?" I ask after a moment to recover.

"Relax," says the man who pulled me in. "We're friends."

I take the chance to take in my supposed saviour. Dusty brown hair, his clothes are simple, utilitarian, the kind of clothes I would wear. Without the military edge that I've come to know these past few days. I relax a little. Both of them are dressed this way. Both seem just a little older than me.

"I'm Alex," he says, "Simon is acting as our chauffeur."

Simon takes a hand off the steering wheel to wave but doesn't turn around.

"More explanations will come soon, we promise. Just know that you're with friends and we've been waiting for you," he says.

The car speeds through a part of the city unknown to me. Streets I don't recognise blur past the window. We pull up outside a large, derelict looking building.

The façade is old; older even than the derelict buildings I'm used to.

"Welcome to the Resistance Bar." We walk down a set of stairs beside the main entrance to the building. It opens up into a large empty space with large support pillars around the room, an old nightclub perhaps. Groups of people are interspersed around the room, and the bar at the end seems to be the main attraction.

"Resistance," he laughs sardonically. "This used to be place for members of the resistance to gather in safety, but these days resistance might as well just describe the friction between factions. It remains, however, neutral ground for any talented. Given the number of talented around, the government has always given it a wide berth as well. You should feel safe here."

Conversations pause as I'm lead through the room, faces turned towards me as all eyes watch. So many young faces, there couldn't be many over 25. Alex leads us to a quiet corner. With relief, we're quickly forgotten about, people going back to whatever conversations they were having, as if it is normal around here for people to come in wearing revealing hospital gowns and covered in blood.

Alex picks up on my body language. "We have some clothes coming for you. Hopefully she isn't too far away," he says. "Simon?"

"No switch," Simon replies.

"You can't see anything?"

"I can't see anything, it's true," Simon says.

"Are you able to use any abilities at all?" Alex directs the question at me.

At that moment, much to my amazement, the semi-familiar old man, the same man shown in the earlier vision, sits down at the table with us. He nods his head toward the other two. "Like I said, she's a Non, no switch, just like her parents," the man says pensively to them. To me he says, "I'm so glad you got out; that these people were able to find you in time. I'm sorry about Aine," he says in a soft voice. His eyes drop in shame. "That's twice now I've let you down. I thought I'd be able to keep you out of this world."

"Twice? We've never spoken before today," I say perplexed.

"I guess you must have been too young to remember. You'd best all get comfortable. This is a long story." He takes a deep breath. "My name is Uri. In the veil war, the first war, your parents had quite the reputation, considered among the most talented psychic soldiers. Certainly the best I ever knew. They were my fiercest adversaries during the first war.

"But then the Templars turned against both sides and the war shifted. The government fell and the Templars and their government puppets took over. Your parents went on to become two of the greatest leaders in the resistance against the new government forces. I became their lieutenant, their closest guard, their protector. And in time their closest friend. Old enemies became close friends. In the time before you were born they were high among the people most wanted by the government. Of course, just like you, they were Nons and by that stage, sadly, they were among the last few left. The Templars were so good at hunting us down.

But your parents were better. Always it seemed one step ahead.

"Then your sister came along. It all changed."

That sentence nails me. "I have a sister?" I ask incredulously.

"Yes. You have a sister," he says,

My heart drops. "A sister?" A question aimed at nobody.

In a daze I slide down into my seat. I don't remember any sister. He waits a moment for me to recover and then continues.

"Then suddenly they had something more important than all that to dedicate their lives to. We tried to get all your family out, we really did. And for a while there it worked. After a while your parents dropped off the government's radar. And it was not long after your sister was born when they were joined by you. You two were all that really mattered to your parents. By then, the resistance ceased to exist in their eyes. I don't blame them. You girls were so beautiful."

"Do you know her name?" I interrupt.

"Claire," he says with a gentle smile. "You really were both such cute kids."

"What happened next?" I ask.

"You need to know that unlike so many of the other abandoneds, your parents didn't actually abandon you. I think you must have been four years old; or... you'd have just turned five. We - the resistance - didn't know where they were. They'd changed everything, taken new identities and moved away from it all. We thought it for the best that we didn't know where they were.

The government seemed to have spies everywhere and so many like your parents had already been found. In the end it didn't help, the government still found them.

"We thought we were protecting you. Instead we failed. At the last moment we got word that the government was closing in on your parents. We found out where they were heading. A group of us hoping to protect your parents arrived just as Templars stormed the place. Your parents had hidden away on a quiet farm. On any other day it would have been quite beautiful. Today it was surrounded with government knights storming across those fields."

He pauses to compose himself for a moment. "Those troops got to your parents first. When we arrived it was too late, but we fought back anyway. They stole Claire away before we could stop them. We fought so hard to get to her. It was the bloodiest battle we had fought in a long while. But they got away. Everyone felt that loss.

"By the time the battle was over, the few of us remaining held the farm and the Templars retreated. And, to my amazement, I found you. Somehow you'd managed to hide yourself unseen under a table. Maybe it was just luck that all of those troops were too stupid to look down to see you. I realised that I still held that promise to protect you, to keep you safe. And the only way I felt I could do that was to keep you at a distance from me while I watched over you. I thought if people worked out the connection between me and you...." He shakes his head. "I guess that was still a mistake. In the end I didn't keep you safe. Twice I've had to learn that lesson."

"Do you know what happened to my sister, to Claire?" I ask tentatively.

"The government have been keeping her captive this whole time, somewhere. I don't know much more than that."

"She's still alive?" I ask hopefully.

"We believe she is. But we've never been able to find her though. They've hidden her too well. And I've always been too worried about leaving you to go looking."

"But you're sure she's alive?"

"I don't know for absolute sure."

I bite my lip. "And my parents?" I ask. I feel like I already know the answer.

His head drops. "They were executed that day," he says.

My heart skips a beat. I nod slowly. "Can you tell me about them? I know nothing about them. I don't even know their names."

He nods. "You've grown up to be so beautiful, so much like your mother, Sari. She was so beautiful, yet so very fierce. A wicked sense of humour and a sharp tongue. Crystal green eyes and vivid red hair just like yours." He smiles, "I really wish I could show you how much you look like her. Your father, Michael, was perhaps the only person capable of balancing your mother. He was the strength behind us all. And very talented. While your mother was the fire of the resistance, the drive behind us, it was his cool head, his planning and ingenuity that kept us alive." His voice trails off, thinking on it further. "Here comes Cara. There's so much more to talk about, so much more I need to tell you. And I'm sure you have a lot of questions, questions about your parents, your talents. But today has been so long and you look like you couldn't stay awake even if you wanted to hear it all. We'll have plenty of time tomorrow to talk about it."

It's true. Just the thought brings a giant yawn, as if needing to prove his point. Quickly stifled the moment Cara walks into view. You know those awkward moments when you find yourself staring at somebody for just that moment too long? It would appear that my eyes have gotten stuck. Roughly my age, her dusty brown hair falls roughly over her ears, with long bangs sweeping down over piercing green eyes, a small nose and a cute heart shaped face with skin pale and lightly freckled. She has the air of somebody who slips through life unaware and uncaring. She is simply and un-assumedly beautiful.

"Hi," she says with a nervous smile and a quick half-wave. "Cara."

My cheeks turn redder than the blood covering me. Does she notice? She looks me up and down and says, "My clothes should fit you. Come with me. You must be anxious to get out of that."

She turns to the others.

"I can't believe you walked her through here wearing nothing more than a hospital gown," she says angrily.

She leads me behind the bar and up a flight of stairs. As we walk up stairs, she says, "I'm sorry they thought it was a good idea to walk you through the crowd of people like that. They don't always think things through. You must be ready to get into some real clothes."

We walk down a long run-down hallway, full of apartment doors. She keeps talking. "This building is one of the safe houses available to talenteds. There's always accommodation for those who need it. But for tonight you can crash in my room."

We stop outside a door near the end of the hallway. Nothing further is said. She fumbles with the key to the room as we stand outside the door; she flashes a smile at me in embarrassment as she struggles to slide the key into the lock. Finally the key cooperates and clicks as the door opens.

Inside is a small studio filled with antique furniture of all kinds and dark earthy colours on the walls. Its appearance is a sharp contrast to the run-down apartment building that surrounds us and the effect is instantly warming. I take the chance to run my fingertips over a set of polished mahogany shelves.

She points. "Through my bedroom is the bathroom. I'll leave you to it. Don't come out until you're feeling human again. I'll have some clothes waiting for you."

♦

The hot water is exquisite. Blood washes off me and drains away the stress of the day. Have I mentioned that the hot water is absolutely divine? I close my eyes and think about nothing else but the feeling of water against my skin. Eventually the water runs clean. Finally I get a chance to switch off for a while. I spend far too long enjoying it.

After drying off, I find a bundle of clothes on the bed, left by Cara, the door to her bedroom closed. On top a bra that's a little small, but passable. Sandy coloured denim pants. A white shirt trimmed in deep red slipped on next. Cara's clothes fit me as if they were my own. Next is a pair of heavy boots, a mix of soft black leather, nylon. I have no idea how but they manage to fit me perfectly, and are instantly the comfiest things I've ever worn. These are some amazing boots.

Last is a soft hooded jacket and, as if to cement the ass kicking image, a pair of leather fingerless gloves, both in matching blood red. It's almost too much.

There's a knock on the door as I try to work out the best way to slip the soldier's long knife I'd taken into the belt of these pants.

"Are you ok in there?" Cara calls in.

"Sure, come in," I reply.

She opens the door and looks me up and down and smiles.

"I thought you'd look good in those gloves, but shit," she says. "How do you like the place?"

I nod. "I love it. It's definitely my style. I wish I could have had a place like this."

Cara's face beams as she says that. "It took me forever to collect this stuff. It's not an easy task to do when you're constantly looking over your shoulder and worried about getting captured by the government."

"I guess it wouldn't be," I respond understandingly. I guess that's the trade-off. One more moment to tie my hair up out of the way and I'm human again. Almost, at least; I can't supress the yawn that follows.

She laughs at me. "Tired?"

"I guess so." My body feels like its run out of energy.

She leans against the door frame to her bedroom. "We don't have to go back downstairs." She pauses a moment too long, watching me. I follow her eyes blink, once, twice, three times.

"You can take the bed if you want. I'll set myself up on the couch," she says.

"No, really, I don't want to impose. This is your place. I'm happy to sleep on the couch."

"It's ok; you really look like you need a good night's sleep."

"I'll survive. It's ok, I don't mind," I say.

Sitting down on the edge of the bed, I sink into the soft mattress. Then I feel the handle of the knife, still tucked into my belt, jab into my side. I'd already forgotten about it. I draw the knife out, deliberately holding its gleaming edge away from me. The inscription 'EX VMBRA IN SOLEM' is written along the face of the blade while there are some numbers, '32:40-42' scratched near the handle.

"Woah," Cara gasps, surprised. "Did you take that from one of the Templars? Where the hell were you hiding that? I'm not sure how I missed that on you before."

I nod to her as I place the knife gingerly on the bed side table. Cara's bed is so soft in comparison to the rock hard mattress I had in the cell while captured. While captured... The events of the past days, each and every little memory hit me like a sledgehammer to the face. My parents are dead. Maybe somewhere out there is a sister I never knew about. Aine is gone. I try to maintain composure, but that only lasts a second. In the end I fail miserably at trying to hold it all in. Tears flow. I'm always stronger than this. Any other day I would be. I try to apologise to Cara. It ends up sounding nothing like "I'm sorry."

She slides onto the bed behind me, wraps her arms around me and rests her head on my shoulder. It's such a gentle gesture, like nothing I'd ever experienced before. Nothing is said. Nothing needed to be said. I lose all sense of time; it could have been hours I spent like this without moving, in the comfort of her arms.

♦

"Wake up, wake up."

Cara is shaking me roughly as she sits up next to me. We must have fallen asleep.

"We've got to leave. We've got to leave now!" her voice shaking.

"What's going on? What's wrong Cara?" I ask sleepily.

"I'm sorry for bringing you here. They're coming. They'll be here any minute. We've got to go. We've got to go now."

"Who's coming?" I'm wide awake now. "Cara you're scaring me."

"This place is supposed to be safe from them. They're coming," she says, her eyes wide open in panic.

They? Government troops? Templars? The realisation turns a switch on in my head. "Are they here?" I ask her.

"Soon. They're close."

"How do you know they're coming?" I ask.

She stops and gives me blank look. "I know."

"Ok, ok." I say. "What's the best way out of here?"

"Come on, we need to get downstairs."

We step out of the studio together. Cara turns back sadly. Her face says we won't be coming back.

I gently take her arm. "Come on, we need to warn everyone."

She nods slowly, building resolve. We run down the hall way, yelling for people to get out, banging on doors. We hit the stairs running, two at a time.

We hit the bottom of the stairs in time to see the front door of the dance floor go flying across the room. Smoke floods through the doorway. Through the smoke come soldiers with guns raised. Cara is half pulling, half dragging me across the room. Guns start firing. Shit.

The exit is only a few short steps from the stairs. To the right are the toilets, forwards through a short hallway is an exit door. Just as I place my hand against the door to push it open, Cara grabs my arm and pulls me into the toilets.

Bang. Just outside the toilets an explosion goes off. Cara motions to me to be quiet. Steps race into the building. Her head nods in rhythm to the beat of boots outside, counting the troops passing by.

"Go. Go now. Outside. Run," she whispers to me.

We burst through the door and aim for the exit. A man behind us shouts. I have no intention of looking back.

Outside the street, only an alley really, is dark; the night not yet complete. At the end of the alley soldiers mill beside a pair of large black vehicles. The white bands on their arms identify them even in this darkness. One of them shouts out, raising the alarm. In a mad rush they all reach for their weapons, unprepared for our presence. I grab Cara's wrist and start running down the alley. Just as we reach the end, she shoves my head down roughly. A fraction of a second later the men are firing on us, bullets flying just inches above where my head used to be. We turn the corner of the alley and are out of their sight. Too close.

We keep on running, running blindly, running scared.

A Stroll through the City

Out of breath we stop finally, finding ourselves in a small park, heavily overgrown with trees. Dawn is breaking over the city. The tree cover offers a decent place to hide for a moment.

"Are you ok? Are you hurt?" I ask Cara.

She shakes her head between deep breaths in.

"Do you know where we are?"

She nods this time.

"Is it safe here?"

"As safe as anywhere I suppose," she says, composing herself.

"We will need to be a little cautious on these streets, this is deep into government friendly territory, but there's a safe house nearby we can head to," she says. "Do you think anybody else got out?"

"Maybe," I shake my head, unsure.

"I should have been faster."

"Faster?"

"If I was better," she breaks, "more talented, more practiced, I don't know, I might have gotten that precog earlier. We could have gotten everyone out sooner."

"You don't know that. You got me out. You got out. Who else could have done better?"

Her look tells me she's not convinced.

"You don't know." I hug her. "How far is it to this safe house?"

"From here? Maybe a 20 minute walk," she says.

"Let's head that way then. You can tell me while we walk how it is that yesterday your friends managed to be outside of that building yesterday to pick me up."

We walk out the trees with a little trepidation, still not sure whether we successfully evaded the soldiers. Between the tree line and the street is a small field of green grass bordered by fence of wooden posts. A flock of crows has set up in the grass catching bugs in the morning dew. As we cross the broken fence line something catches my eye. On a wooden post not 50 metres away sits a crow looking directly at me. It's the blackest bird I've ever seen. Cara must have noticed me stop because she asks me what I'm looking at.

"I swear that there's a crow over there watching us," I say.

She looks over in the direction I was facing. "What crow?"

"That one over..." I don't get to finish the sentence. The bird is gone.

"I guess I'm just over paranoid at the moment," I say.

"Don't blame you," she says with a sigh. "Don't blame you at all."

We walk together in silence for a while. Cara leads me through a number of narrow city streets. I'm totally lost. The warmth of the new dawn's light fights this cold concrete maze as best it can. The feeling of panic from the earlier escape has been replaced with weariness.

Cara breaks the silence. "Uri came to us, maybe a week ago and told us what had happened to you. He's old resistance, just like he said, but has been out of the game for a while. He said that he'd been watching out for you. Then he told us who you were. Your parents are pretty legendary among the new resistance.

"We brought in Alex to locate you. And he did. And he told us where you were. And we really struggled to think about how we were going to be able to help him, help you. That place you came out of, that 'hospital', is filled with the worse of government types. Hell, we didn't believe you'd still be alive. That morning though I had a precog of you. I saw you running out of the hospital. And I knew we had to find you. Once I explained the precog to them, it was pretty easy to convince them that somebody should wait around the front of the building for you. I'm glad they hung around waiting for you. I'm not sure how long I could have lasted waiting in front of a government building like that. And then yeah, here we are."

She stops suddenly, her eyes inquiring. "How did you get out of there, anyway?"

"I'm still not sure... I had help I guess. Someone, something helped get me out. I don't know how to explain it. It was like this entity, this ghost, stepped out of the shadows and freed me. It was... violent." The question brings back memories. They seem distant, strange; though it was only yesterday, it seems like it was years ago.

My answer gives Cara a worried look, but she says nothing further. We keep wandering, in silence.

There is a lot more activity in this part of the city on these streets than I'm used to. Cara says, "We need to be careful what we say from this point forward, none of these people will be sympathetic. They've all been trained for years by the government to hand us over if there's the slightest suspicion against us."

"Couldn't they just have other talented people going around looking for people like us?" I ask.

"The Templars have always been absolutely anti-talent. They'd never trust a talented person for something like that," she responds.

"There was one with them when I was taken."

"You sure?"

I nod. "Absolutely. I think she was there to identify what switch we were, kind of like what Simon was trying to do."

"A construct programmer then?"

"I guess."

She shrugs. "Hey, are you hungry?" she asks.

My stomach rumbles its response loudly. My last meal was the scraps I was fed while captured.

"Hah, thought so," Cara says.

"I, ah, don't have any way of getting food," I say, embarrassed.

"I've got you covered," She laughs as she tries to assure me with a gentle touch on my arm. Instead it's like a lightning bolt through me. I'm hyperaware of the sensation of her fingertips against my skin. "It's not a problem."

She pulls me into the nearest food place, a café of sorts with seating on the street.

"Order whatever you want," she says.

Breakfast is a simple bacon and egg roll. It's quite frankly the best thing I've ever tasted. Such foods are a luxury we never got much of in the abandoned parts of the city.

"They don't have stuff as good as this where I'm from. The people selling food there are pretty terrible." I laugh.

A few stray looks from strangers suggests this was an unusual thing to say. I drop it.

"How old you Cara?" I ask.

"Twenty, you?"

"Something like that."

"Why?"

I shrug, "Just wondering."

"Everyone seems so young, why's that?"

Her eyes go wide. She leans over to whispers to me. "Not here." She leans back from a moment, then swears under her breath. "Shit. Cops."

We both put on our best look of innocence. The next moments are spent nervously. The police both just smile at us and move on. Not an issue in the end. We watch them, perhaps a little too attentively, as they cross the street.

"Perhaps it's time to get out of here?" she suggests.

"Good idea," I say.

"Come on then, the place we're heading isn't far from here."

I follow Cara out of the café. We pause a moment as Cara battles with unruly item of clothing, her loose shirt and belt buckle locked in mortal combat. Across the street from us the cops have stopped in place, in intense discussion. He turns in our direction and points.

I grab Cara's wrist. "Time to be somewhere else."

She looks up to see what I'm talking about.

"Shit," she swears, nailing the sentiment.

This is becoming a habit. We both bolt. Thankfully the street is still reasonably quiet this early in the morning. Nobody seems willing to get in our way. Mostly they stand and stare at us; all wearing the same shallow, stupefied expression. Have they never seen somebody run from the police before?

"Left! Left!" Cara yells about 100 metres down from the cafe. We take the left up a short set of stairs, jump onto a concrete garden edge, over a small garden and through the middle of a small section of green space.

Beyond that, a concrete wall confronts us, as tall as I am. I flash Cara an uncertain look as we cut through the grass field. I don't know if we can make this. She doesn't stop. We hit it side by side, hands grasping the ledge; the concrete is rough, painfully so, under my hands. Scrapped elbows provide the necessary leverage.

A hand grabs at my left ankle as I lean over the top. That earns my pursuer a sharp kick with the heel of my boot before I roll rather ungracefully over the top. Really need to stop with these close calls.

We land together into a narrow alley. The drop on the other side is further than implied by the climb and I land awkwardly, pain shooting up through my left knee. Cara takes my arm and steadies me as I stumble away from the wall. A quick look behind as we reach the end of the alley shows that we haven't seemed to be followed over the wall. Not willing to wait around to find out.

"It's not far from here," Cara says as we take off again.

We take another few turns before Cara directs me down a narrow side alley. On the other side it opens out into a dark street, itself not much wider than the alley. The sun hasn't visited this street for a long while, the air icy cold. The street itself is lined with rubbish skips and heavy security doors. No wall remains untouched by graffiti.

Past two buildings, Cara leads the way down into an underground car park. Strip lighting offer little illumination. Everything is a monotone grey turned ever-so green, walls free of the graffiti that decorates the street above. The area is larger than expected with at least twenty available car parks. Towards the rear is a thick steel door next to which three dark navy delivery vans are parked in parallel. Each is unmarked. Each tinted beyond visibility. I'm less than convinced that this place is as safe as the term safe-house presumably is meant to imply. The rest of the car park is empty; with nothing to absorb the sound our footsteps echo loudly.

"I should warn you," Cara says, "we might not be entirely welcome here."

Because that's really what I wanted to hear.

"This is a kine safe-house. They'll give us sanctuary, no issue. At least, long enough to let the heat die down a little," She continues, "but, kines tend to keep to their own kind, they're distrustful of others. They tend to be, aggressive. A little too pushy, hot-headed. The shoot first, ask questions later types, you know?" Cara looks at me to see if I'm following.

"At least we keep out of other people's business." The short and sharp inflection comes from a man waiting in the doorway.

He is dressed with military simplicity. A plain tight fitting shirt, navy blue, covers a muscular frame, with matching cargo pants and black military boots completing the picture. If it wasn't for the fact his blonde hair is too long, he would fit in well with any of the other soldiers already met.

"Erik." Cara's tone reflects both recognition and contempt.

"Cara." Erik succeeds in outdoing her contempt.

It would appear that these two are thrilled to see each other.

"Word of what happened at the bar is spreading quickly. Still, of all the places you could take her, you brought her here?" he says shaking his head.

He looks towards me. He doesn't look impressed.

"You'd both better come in," he says. To Cara he whispers rather unsubtly, "You shouldn't have brought her here."

We're lead up a flight of stairs. The building inside is modern hotelesque; clean white walls and cheap forgettable paintings. Down a twisting hallway we come to a man doing his best impression of a statue, standing in front of an otherwise random door.

We step into a war room. Around the room are more people with clothes matching Erik's; a mixture of men and women, twelve in total. Each of them shares his stoic expression. Each occupies a position around a long boardroom table. Three large black sports bags sit on the table in front of them, spilling out a large number of automatic weapons.

"What's going on?" Cara asks with a worried look on her face.

"As far as we know, there are still government soldiers at the Resistance bar. We also believe they're still holding everyone there, presumably while they work out what to do with them. We intend to hit back quickly. Clean up the mess you've left as best we can," Erik says.

As if to re-enforce just how they intend to do that, he takes a submachine gun from a bag and loudly works the cocking handle. The motion is less than subtle.

He continues, "Stay out of our way while we prepare. In the next room are some others who made it out, along with some food and drink if you want it."

His attention turns back to his preparation.

◆

Cara and I follow the hall way along to the next room. The door opens smaller studio; bed, kitchen & living room cramped into one room. A woman sits on the bed reading a paperback. On a tiny small couch a young man is reading a small novel. Neither is older than 25. Both look up from their books and watch us as we come through the door.

"Two.... Only two people made it out?" Cara says devastated.

The woman's face reflects Cara's despair.

"There may have been more. We're the only ones that came here. Perhaps others went elsewhere. I'm not sure," the woman says.

"But this is the closest safe-house to the bar. Only two people..." she says lowering herself to the edge of the bed in shock.

I sit down beside her on the bed and wrap an arm around here, pulling her close.

"You're not responsible for what happened," I try to reassure her. It doesn't seem to help much.

"Hey, at least you got out," the man says.

On the bed, the woman's eyes light up in panic. She shakes her head, to say that that was the wrong thing to say.

I take hold of Cara's wrist and lift her chin up softly with the back of my hand so that I can look her in the eyes. "There's nothing more you could have done. We don't have long before we have to leave again and I still have lots of questions. I still have no idea how I even work. Hell, I such a bare idea of what the veil really is I just don't understand how it could be so important to what I am."

She nods slowly, composing herself somewhat.

The man gets up from the couch, leaving the book open. "We can probably help with that a little more than she will be able to. Cara's talent is just a little too innate for her to be able to teach properly," he says. "It happens or it doesn't, as she is unfortunately aware. We're a little different."

He grabs a pair of soft drink cans from a small bar bridge. He gives me one and tries to offer Cara another. When she doesn't respond, he just shrugs and keeps it himself.

"Theo." He holds out his hand to shake.

Reluctantly I return the greeting. As our hands touch I feel snakes of energy wrap themselves up my arm. I recoil in horror. He laughs at my reaction.

"Behave yourself Theo. She's clearly new to this," the woman says.

"Oh, don't be so sour," he counters.

She just gives him a scolding look in return.

"And my name is Melita, and it's a pleasure to finally meet you," she says with a smile.

"You know who I am?"

"When Uri came to the bar with the news that Sari and Michael's daughter had been captured that day word spread pretty quickly," she says. "If you couldn't tell, Theo here manipulates energy and builds constructs. And is more than willing to remind you how rare his talent is. Though," she looks at him and says, "I think she might have you beat. I, on other hand, am a telepath. Between us we should be able to fill in a few of those gaps in your understanding. Maybe, if what Uri said of you is true, we might even be able to teach you a few things. And, despite his other faults, when it comes to energy constructs, Theo is a very good teacher."

Theo drags a small arm chair in front of the end of the bed.

"Cool, energy constructs 101, abridged edition," he says with an unnatural exuberance.

He holds out his hand to me, palm up with fingers spread as if he were holding a bowl up.

"I want you to wave your hand over mine and tell me what you feel."

As my hand moves over his, the air starts to feel thicker, my skin tingles as if moving through cool fog.

"You feel it?" he asks. "Your basic energy ball. You can't see it, it has no mass of its own, but your body still reacts to it in the only way it knows how, tactility. That's how your body will react and feedback a lot of the information it needs to when working with energy. Eventually it becomes like another limb with the same sensations you'd get from any other limb."

I nod. That's exactly what the entity made me experience before.

"Now, it's all well and good to get basic feedback, of the sort, but to actually manipulate it with any level of complexity, it needs to be something a little more visual."

Melita interrupts, "Not everyone one is visual."

"True, but most people are. Let's assume she is and go from there," he says. "Now like I said, energy is invisible to the naked eye, but," he leans over and taps me a little too hard on the side of my head, "our minds can compensate for that too. I hope you have a good imagination. The next bit draws a fine line between imagination and reality, so the better the imagination - the better people tend to be at this."

I assure him my imagination is just fine.

"Ok, I want you to close your eyes but I want you to keep a visual of the room around you in your mind, as if your eyes where still open. As you turn your head around the picture in your mind should show you what you'd expect to see. Got it? It's important that the visual is first person, yeah. Don't go wandering off around the room. That's another lesson."

I nod. "It's dark but I think I have it pictured."

"Yeah, of course it's dark. Your eyes are closed silly. Now, look down to where my hand is."

Strange, despite the fact that his hand has moved, I can see an outline of it easily in my head.

"Good, now watch."

It's faint, difficult to see at first in the darkness of my mind, but in his hand an orb appears. It starts first as tendrils of fluorescent light of indescribable colour that slowly spin out of his palm, forming a small bowl shape before growing upwards until they complete the sphere. It's difficult to describe what it looks like. There simply aren't sufficient words. I open my eyes in amazement.

"I take it from your reaction that you can see what I'm talking about. Good. You've experienced something that only other energy manipulators get to, something Melita and Cara here can't." He seems to be smiling at me in genuine pleasure.

"The easiest way I've found to manipulate energy is to picture the world around you in your head, overlay what you want to happen in that picture and with a little extra push your mind fills in the rest.

"Now it's your turn. Before we start, one thing that is important to be aware of. When you 'look' at somebody like you are doing with me at the moment, when you connect with another person, called scanning, it's considered quite invasive. While a light touch is often used as a greeting, anything more than that is kind of like having somebody watch you in the shower, except for the fact that it's quite obvious."

A sentence forms in my head. A voice, Melita's, reads them out, "Of course, that doesn't stop them."

"I saw that. Ironically, a telepath transmitting directly to a person without permission is considered much worse," Theo bites back.

"Bah, we're teaching here," Melita says.

"Hmm, speaking of scanning, perhaps we should have done it sooner. Did you know that there's somebody else is connected to you? We all tend to have faint but constant bonds to the people most important to us. It's an empathic link. For instance, you have the beginnings of a bond forming between you and Cara. This, however, is a much more solid. But I thought though that your parents were, ah, dead," he says awkwardly. "Do you have any other family or a love interest perhaps?"

Cara finally breaks her silence. "She only just found out yesterday that she might have a sister somewhere that she didn't know about. They haven't been together for at least fifteen years."

"Hmm, maybe. It's possible, but it seems like a bit of stretch. Anybody else close, a lover perhaps?" he asks.

I shake my head. "No lovers." I don't know who he might be referring to.

"Then I'm not sure, it's doesn't look like a trace, definitely has the feeling of old familiar bond. It could very well be your sister. Probably best to keep an eye on it but we can come back to it. It doesn't seem to be going anywhere," Theo says. "Ok, back to energy constructs 101. First we need to teach you how to draw on energy from across the veil, then how to control and condense it into something usable. Close your eyes again and relax your arms. As you practice, the next steps will come quicker and with less thought, but for the first time, we do things the hard way. When moving energy, you need to become both a storage container and a conduit for it. I want you to imagine yourself as a hollow glass statue; picture it such that if you were to look down at your hands right now, all you'd see is glass. It's a simple enough image for your mind to imply a storage container. The next bit is part instinctual, so we'll have to see how we go. Don't worry if you don't get it at first. Are you with me so far?"

I nod, eyes closed.

"Ok, then now is a good time to talk about what the veil is. We live here, in this physical..." He pauses to search for a word. "...reality, I suppose. Yeah?"

"I guess so," I answer.

"Well, overlaid over this reality are an infinite number of other, pure energy dimensions, I guess, dimension isn't the right word for it, but it's a difficult concept to describe. It is an infinite number of pure energy universes that are overlaid over our reality. They also hold an infinite memory of everything that has ever happened or will ever happen, as it is at least from the energy side of the equation. That's how Cara's precognition talent works. Her talent peels the layers back to get to a memory of a universe to be, and her mind converts this into something she can interpret, a memory or vision.

"The veil is the barrier between this reality and those other dimensions. It keeps us separated. Though, people tend to refer to both the barrier and the universes it separates collectively as the veil. When we use energy, we make small tears through this barrier and tap into the energy on the other side, pulling it through the barrier for our use. At least, that's the mechanics of it. In practice, it's a lot more instinctual and a lot less dramatic.

"Do you still have the glass statue pictured in your mind?"

I nod. It's a lie. I quickly reimagine it.

"Good, being able to hold onto an idea, a plan, in your head during distractions is important. Now, I want you to picture yourself, as this hollow glass statue, filling up with fluid. It should pour into you; concentrate on the colour, focus on the texture of it."

As he talks, I can picture in my mind my body filling with this liquid, a velvety thickness. It's dark,

55

blacker than darkness of my mind. A dark fog leaches from me. Where it pools in the statue of my mind, in my hands and my feet, my body reciprocates. It weighs heavy inside me. My skin tingles with it. My heart races with the sensation.

"Wow. Are you seeing this?" Theo exclaims.

"I've... never seen anything like it before," Melita is just as excited.

I open my eyes to all three staring at me, three pairs of wide eyes. The feeling is lost. It's unnerving.

"What?" I wonder what's going on.

"That was..." he struggles for his words, "none of us have ever seen anything like it."

"What?" I ask again, more insistently. Their attention has made me suddenly very nervous.

"Come on, focus. Eyes closed," Theo says. "Let's try this again."

I close my eyes again. "Glass statue, fluid filling it up, got it."

I feel velvet fluid pour through me again, sensation filling every limb. Before long I'm struggling to picture myself through the fog in my mind, my body, my statue unclear as it fills completely. My heart is racing.

"Hold it, hold onto that feeling. Don't open your eyes just yet," Theo says rapidly. "Hell, that's frickin cool."

"I think I'm full," I say unsure.

"We can tell," Cara says, from further away than expected.

"Ok, ok, now to condense it," Theo says. "It's not particularly useful in the form it's in at the moment.

The liquid, the fluid is just that, fluid. It flows easily but it's too difficult to shape in that form and that's what we're trying to achieve."

I'm struggling to maintain myself, my body tense with the sensation.

"Keep concentrating. It gets easier," Theo assures me. "Left or right handed?"

"Left," Cara answers for me. I didn't realise she'd noticed.

"Ok. The next step is to take all that fluid in your body and picture it flowing up into your left arm. You want to squish it all in there as best as it will fit. It'll condense."

The weight leaves my body and grows in my arm. My arm feels heaver still. The sensation as the fluid flows into my arm is electrifying. It's intoxicating.

"Good," he says, "you're starting to get more control, even this quickly. You're a quick learner. Now we condense it again. With a little bit of practice, you'll be able to skip straight to this step. Take the fluid from before and compress it further until it's only filling your hand. And keep those eyes closed. You're doing well."

As the fluid condenses in my hand, the sensation over my skin goes beyond just tingling. My hand feels like it's coursing with electricity. The weight grows further still. It's difficult to resist the temptation to open my eyes though. I can tell Melita has shifted on the bed, her attention completely on me now. Theo feels closer too.

"Now for the most important step, forming it. Remember the energy orb I created before? You're going to do the same. Hold your hand up like I did, palm up, fingers stretched. This time, rather than use the same glass statue metaphor, just picture the sphere in your mind, then flow all the fluid to fill it. Metaphors like the hollow glass statue help lay the framework to build, to construct something, to teach your mind what it needs to do, but they aren't entirely necessary. Hold onto the memory of what you're feeling right now."

I can feel something resembling a ball sitting in my hand. It's soft and fluffy, and while it also feels dense, it sits lightly in the palm of my hand. In my head, the despite in being pitch black, the orb is glowing with fluorescence. It's a surreal vision.

"Ok, this is too amazing," Theo says. "I want you to keep concentrating on that image in your head, but you can open your eyes when you're ready."

I slowly open up my eyes. In my upturned palm is a sphere matching the vision in my head. Dark, too black though slightly transparent, it fills my hand completely. The smoky surface ebbs and flows while black tendrils bleed off it, obscuring the spherical shape somewhat. My hand is also leaking the same soft smoky substance. It makes my hand look like it is on fire, were it not for the fact that somebody forgot to tell it that fire isn't black. I've never seen anything like it. The sphere starts to grow less dense.

"Hold it. Keep concentrating."

Melita is shaking her head. "I've never seen a visible construct."

"The next step is to do all that, eyes open. It's not particularly useful if we'd have to close our eyes and sit and concentrate all the time, is it?"

"From this point forward, you're only limited by your imagination. While this silly sphere seems useless in itself, anything you might build uses the same simple process."

Somebody knocks heavily on the door. The unwelcome distraction steals my focus completely; the sphere in my hand dissipates quickly.

Erik walks into the room.

"We're leaving in ten," he says. "Given that none of us are going to remain here, I'd really recommend not hanging around. This place won't be safe and you especially," he looks directly at me, "shouldn't risk it alone here."

"Can we go with you?" Cara asks Erik.

"You want to go back?" I say surprised.

"I have to know if people are ok. Maybe grab a few personal things."

"There's no room in any of the vehicles," Erik says.

"I'll be able drive them," Theo says.

"But we walked here," Melita says.

Theo raises an eyebrow, to suggest that that isn't an issue.

Erik thinks for a moment. Eventually he nods. "Ok. I don't think it's a good idea but I can't really stop you. Make sure you stay out of the way of my team."

"Thank you," Cara says.

He turns and disappears back down the hallway.

Melita turns to me. "Right well, quick lesson in telepathy then. Start off by thinking of the person you want to connect with. Kind of like the constructs lesson, to connect with another person you need to imagine a link forming between you and them. Then add that little bit extra, that extra push like what you did with the orb. It's a little hard for me to describe since it happens so effortlessly for us. I'm not sure how it's going to work for you.

"It's up to you as to how you chose to imagine the link. People use all sorts of personal metaphors. It also helps a lot if you know where the person is. Since the link still traverses physical space, it helps to be able to push it in the right direction. Once you have the connection, it simply a matter of pushing things onto it or pulling things from it. If you're communicating politely, it's best to picture putting what it is you want to send about here. In the less polite cases you need to be a little more forceful and there's a lot more that hasn't been covered, like shielding, but that's the gist of it."

She waves her hand closely in front of her forehead. "A person communicating politely with you will do the same, so that thoughts and words will sit just in front of your eyes. It's why we go all, blank stare into the distance, when communicating with each other. Like pretty much any other ability, intent helps shape in your mind what you want to communicate, all it takes then is a little more omph and you make it happen. Get it?"

I'm not sure I truly understand, but perhaps it'll come with time. I'm distracted by other thoughts.

Whether heading back to the bar is really a good idea, whether Cara notices the way her body is touching mine. I nod my head anyway; it seems like the appropriate thing to do.

"Time to go," Erik yells down the hallway.

Melita gives me an unexpected kiss goodbye on the cheek. "Stay safe cutie. You'll get it," she says overly friendly. "Find me again soon because there's a lot more I teach you."

A Friend Indeed

"Stay safe cutie," Cara jibes with a poke to the shoulder. She grins at me.

"What? Jealous?"

The three parked vans sit open, as they are packed with gear by the twelve from the safe-house. Split evenly around each van, they work quickly to load what appears to be an excessive amount of gear. Still despite their well-rehearsed manner, the automatic weapons hanging on their shoulders are checked and double-checked and triple-checked. Everyone appears anxious.

"Keep close behind," Erik says to Theo. "We'll let you know when it's safe to enter the building. Once you're inside, we'll give you a few minutes to grab whatever you can carry. There'll be no going back after that."

"Follow me," Theo says to Cara and me.

Still within sight of the car park entrance, Theo walks us down the street a little way, sliding his hand along each of the cars we walk pass. He stops us next to a dark coupe.

"You think they would have learned after war," he says, checking up and down the street. "With these electronic locks, it makes it simple."

He presses his hand flat against the coupe's door, his eyes glazing over for a moment. Smiling broadly he rotates his hand and with a click the door opens. He waves for us to get in.

"This isn't your car, is it?" I ask Theo as Cara climbs in next to me.

He just grins as the car comes to life, the soft whir of its electric motor the only sound in the cabin. Car tyres squeal as Theo floors it to catch up with the vans as they go speeding down the road. The unfamiliar city streaks by, uninteresting. Daydreams allure. A dull palette of grey and brown; her electric touch so intense. The way her lips slip against mine...

Cara screams.

"Oh no," she mutters to herself. The colour drains from her face, her gaze distant terror. She curls up, a quivering ball of fear on the seat beside me.

"What's wrong?" I ask Cara, afraid of what it might be.

All she can do is shake her head. The convoy comes to a halt outside the front of the building encompassing the bar. The place appears to be devoid of any soldiers. The twelve pour from the vans with weapons raised and storm into the bar in groups of four.

"Stay in the car." Theo yells to us, jumping out. He takes up watch at the building entrance.

I slide next to Cara and wrap her up in my arms and enfold her against me. My attempt at comfort unsure;

something I've never been terribly good at it. Left behind, we wait in silence broken only by the crying of Cara cradled softly against my shoulder. Nothing can be heard from what is happening inside the building.

Out the car window I notice a flock of crows occupying a brick wall half a block down the street. I count eight, eight dark omens waiting patiently.

One in particular sits and watches back and I swear it's that same one as earlier, following me around. What a curious thought. What are you foreshadowing little bird?

Erik and the three others of his team solemnly step out from the building. All are shaking their heads. They wait by the entrance while Erik walks across to us.

"We were too late..." he says, letting the sentence trail off. "We did capture two soldiers who'd remained behind to search for intel but the rest had already left." He pauses to collect himself. "It's, ah, it's not good in there. You really don't want to go inside. I can have people bring stuff out, name it. It's just, there are things in there you don't want to see."

"There's nothing in there for me," I say.

Cara lets go of me and pushes herself out of the car. Her face a blank mask showing none of the emotion of half a minute ago.

"I've seen it, I know I go in. There is no avoiding it."

I can't read her face. What is she thinking?

"It's not that I want to," she says, her voice quivering. "I really don't."

She looks at me, her glance a question in hope that I'll join her. Erik's downward gaze suggests something else entirely. I nod, taking her arm. Whatever it is that she's seen, I'll follow. We step down the stairs in tandem.

The room is dark. Erik guides us quickly but firmly towards the stairway at the rear of the room. Beyond the directive shoulder in front of me are the rest of the twelve, standing closely together across the room with their backs to us. Before them are two government soldiers on their knees; both easily identified by the distinguishing white arm bands. They seem calm despite their situation. Two men stand over of them, guns pointed at their heads. One is yelling, a lot. Something about where the others are. Neither captive speaks. Given the level of frustration showing on the face of the yelling man, it appears that neither captive will cooperate.

Beside me Cara folds, falling to her knees. A sob slips from her. My heart drops, the cause of her reaction now apparent. To the right of the captive solders are a number of bodies lying on the ground. From where I stand, it's too dark to see who it might be. Before I can help Cara up, she's on her feet again. She shoves Erik out of the way, running towards them. I follow her before I realise. I wish I hadn't.

Before her lie five bodies. All have had their throats slit, blood still slick in a large pool around them. Shit. Alex is the first person I identify. Simon lies beside him. The next two I never met, though I remember them being at the bar last night. The last body is Uri. His face is heavily swollen, as if he was beaten before he was killed. The only connection I had with my parents, my

65

sister, whatever life I had before the streets, gone. The loss sinks in.

Hah, here five people lie dead and yet all I can think of is how it affects me. I feel strangely calm about that. Cara is hysterical, held back by Erik. She struggles. I wrap my arms tenderly around her and cradle her head against my body. She hits me, screaming. Her fists beat against my shoulder. And I let her, let her get it out. The adrenaline shows it in slow motion.

Eventually she breaks down, sobbing into my neck.

Erik meets my eyes. He understands.

"You've got 5 minutes upstairs before we have to leave this place. We can't hang around here. Take what you can. Be quick," he says.

With one arm around her waist to support her, I lead Cara upstairs. She just shuffles blankly along with me. The door to her room is open. Inside, the place looks ransacked.

"Come on, you must have stuff here you want to take?"

Instead, she sits on the edge of the bed and stares blankly out the door. Ok. I wander around the room looking for anything that seems like it might be important to her. I don't do well, a few trinkets, a book. Mostly it's the furniture she spent so much time collecting that strikes me as most important to her. Hopefully one day she'll be able to start again.

In my final pass around the room I come across the soldier's knife I'd left lying on the table. Isn't it amazing how the span of a single day can feel like a lifetime? With no place to put the knife, I can only carry it in hand. That's going to make for some interesting conversation.

With nothing obvious left to collect I sit down next to Cara. I've nothing to say. I'm terrible with situations like this. In the end we just stay like this for a minute in silence. She looks at me and nods. Grief gives way to solemnity. She takes from me what I collected and leaves them on the bed. She doesn't look back as we step out the room, perhaps for the final time.

It's difficult to stop myself from looking towards the bodies as we walk towards the door. Did they blame me for their deaths? Were their last thoughts of hatred towards me? What have I done to cause this?

"You cannot run forever, little one. We will find you," the captive on the left yells at me, staring directly at me. He makes an attempt to stand up. The man standing over him reaches a hand out, palm forward. I feel as much as see the concussive force hit the captive in the chest. He falls backwards. With a foot planted firmly on his chest, the captor leans over the soldier and draws a gun. It fires, the sound echoing around the room. And he dies. Nothing dramatic. It's over faster than my mind can comprehend.

The other prisoner reacts instantly. Too quick for his own captor, the prisoner pushes past the team surrounding them. He's almost at me before I realise he's moved. They all react far too slowly. In other circumstances I might consider it comical how easily they let it happen. In other circumstances. With only a few metres between us, none of them will stop him reaching me.

A stride away from me he stops. A rivulet of blood follows the knife as I pull it out of his neck. Moments before my mind was filled with images of blood flowing from him, abstract in their hyperrealism. With just that thought in my mind it was easy to work out what was going to happen next. I knew. Yet knowing what was going to happen I still felt powerless to deviate from the path fate laid out for me. I didn't want this. Or did I? Correction; I shouldn't want this. And yet consider those with throats slashed. Did they deserve their fate? This man surely deserves his. It's easy to justify what I've done.

Blood flows from the gaping wound I opened in his neck. He stands frozen before me, his face one of confusion. The room dims. Before I can stop myself, I'm burying the knife in him again. Again and again, I can't stop myself. Arms reach under my armpits and pull me back. A firm hand holds my wrist. I fight the restraint; still I try to continue stabbing the man. At some point the knife is forced from me.

"It's enough. You did well," Erik says.

The faces around me turn from shock to celebratory smiles. That doesn't seem right. What's to celebrate?

Erik shrugs. "We were hoping to get a bit more information from them before that, but..." I tune out of anything else he says, my thoughts lost to the chaotic violence. I have to get out of here. This room is stifling, walls crushing me, the light dims. I run outside and straight into Theo.

"Hey, are you ok?" he asks.

"What now?" I shake my head.

"If Erik and his team are heading back to the safe house then you should probably go back with them, at least for now. Work out what you want to do from there where it's safe. We'll head back once everything is wrapped up inside."

That wasn't the question I asked. I go and lean against the car and wait. Wait for Erik's team to wrap up. Wait to face Cara. Wait for the world to stop spinning. Waiting isn't such a fantastic idea, with hindsight.

Ten long minutes it takes them to come out. Plenty of time to think about what I've done. It bothers me I couldn't stop myself. It should bother me more than it does.

Erik leads Cara from the building and over to me.

"You don't want to hang around for this next bit," he says. "Oh and this belongs to you."

The Templar's knife slides out of the sheath he hands me, its handle sitting familiar in my grip. Its blade mirror polished once again. I don't want to know where it came from. The sheath fastens to my belt as if it belongs there.

Theo takes Cara by the shoulders and guides her into the back of the car. I slide in beside her once she's settled and sit there uncertain, torn between emotions, second guessing everything.

My corvine watcher sits perched on the distant wall the only bird remaining. I guess their job is done. We watch each other, he on his seat and me on mine. Does he know what I've done? Does he sit there judging me? Hurry and play your part.

The car starts and we drive away. My stalker recedes and with him the last memory of innocence.

A Walk in the Park

The drive back to the safehouse is sullen. There have been enough lessons for today. We're the last to drive into the underground parking lot of the safe-house. One van is empty, the door into the building open. The rest are open as people unload. I open my car door and am half out the door when an explosion in the building rips through the silence. It's followed by the sound of sporadic automatic gunfire. A member of Erik's team comes running out of the building. She's covered in blood. Smoke follows her out the door.

"It's a trap! It's a bloody trap!" She screams.

The squeal of tyres can be heard on the street above. Suddenly the car park explodes into activity, people running everywhere.

Erik screams at our car, to Theo, "Get them the hell out of here. Go!"

More automatic weapons start adding themselves to the cacophony. Cara grabs an arm and pulls me into the car. Theo punches the accelerator and I'm flung awkwardly over Cara. My feet touch the roof while my face is down between Cara's knees, looking at the footwell. I've looked better. The sound of the car flooring it through the car park echoes hollow.

"How did they find this place?" Theo asks. "Hell girl, what the fuck have you brought down on us?"

Crunch. The car hits something hard, steel on steel. The impact hurls me violently against the forward seats. My shoulder hits something awkwardly, plastic and steel digging into me. It hurts. The pain doesn't stop. I have no idea what's going on outside.

Arms guide me back onto the seat. I'm not sure I'm glad to finally be able to see out the window. Behind us soldiers stand around vehicles sub machine guns pointed in our direction. We haven't travelled more than 50 metres down the road yet we're facing the wrong direction. Smoke rises up from the bonnet. The rear windscreen shatters as the soldiers open fire. Theo swears.

"Get ready to run for it. This car isn't going to get us much further. Be ready," he yells at us.

We make the end of the street, no further. The car's wheels lock up as one of the damaged engines grinds itself to a halt. It slides sideways into the intersection.

Theo is out of the car instantly. He stands in the doorway and draws a small handgun I didn't know he had, shooting back at the soldiers over the car roof. At this distance, there are no quivering barn-doors.

"Run you fools. Get the hell out of here!" he yells back at us.

We don't need to be told twice. Here we are, running again. Any direction will do.

"I know a place we can go," Cara says as we run. "We need to work out what the hell is happening."

●

Cara leads me to a large fenced off block holding nothing but an overgrown forest. The sign at the entrance marks it as the city botanical gardens.

"I used to come here all the time growing up," she says. "I would to spend days in here. It's been untended since the war so it's a little overgrown but I think that might work to our advantage if we need somewhere to hide. At the very least there are so many hidden tracks through here that you could lose anybody if you needed to."

She walks me down a winding pathway, heavily shaded by the forest growing overhead. We settle underneath a large fig tree that looks over an overgrown grass field, the remains of a crumbling picnic hut distinguishable in front of us. There isn't another person in sight.

"How are you feeling?" I get the courage to ask her.

"Hungry I guess," she says, dodging the question.

"How are you really feeling?" I push.

She shuffles up next to me and lays her head into my neck. "Torn. Irreparable. I want to feel sad for them, but I can't. I can't accept it. And then there's you, I wish we could have met under better circumstances. My world is crumbling around me and I want to help you but I'm not sure how long I can do this before I fall apart. You deserve better. I know you want to find your sister and I want to help you. But I'm not sure how much longer I can keep this up until I unravel."

"You've given me enough. I can't ask for more. You don't have to follow me. I only see it getting worse," I say.

At that moment, her resolve visibly hardens. She leans back from me, eyes red but alert. She sits there a moment, just looking at me.

"I'm not sure what I can do to help, but I'm in. You stood by me and I'll stand by you. I know what I'm getting into," she says, "but I'm not sure where we start."

"And that's where I come in," a voice says, accented mildly Irish, out of nowhere despite us being alone. "Do you have any idea how long I've waited for you to slow down?"

"What the hell?" I exclaim, looking around for the source of the voice.

I'm ready to bolt, before I see the cause of my alarm. On a branch above us sits half a metre of exceptionally black crow. My stalker. Up close it's easy to see she's far from your typical crow. Her feathers lack the iridescence hues of a normal crow; so pitch black that it's impossible to make out individual vanes. Hell, she's so black it's difficult to focus on her at all. Then there are the faint red eyes, the only identifiable feature. Faint black vapor seeps from her. It makes her appear scorched.

She takes notice of the confused look I give her. "I upset somebody once. It's a long story."

"It talks..." Cara looks stunned.

"*She* talks."

"You're a construct?" I ask.

"Err, no, not really," she responds. "It would be closer to say I'm *your* construct, but the way you use the word 'construct' isn't correct. It definitely doesn't tell the whole story."

"Wait, hold up. I'm talking to a bird and it's talking back."

"As if that's the craziest thing that's happened to you today," she says. "You'll have to imagining me shrugging here. Birds can't really do that you know, even the talking ones."

"What are you then? Do you have a name?" I ask.

"Again, picture me shrugging. What do you want to call me? I am an omen of death. Something you have a lot of experience with lately. You could say that you are the harbinger of death. Thus, I am you. Or yours, there isn't any difference from my point of view, but I think it might help you if think of it that way. Hmmm, perhaps that's a bit too dramatic."

"You are me?" I ask confused.

"You, yours, yes. I'm not a construct though, I was never constructed. I am an intelligent being. I guess I look like a construct in your world though. One day you'll wonder if there is a difference. No idea on that by the way. Still, we're not here to discuss philosophy, no? I've been called a lot of things before, but if you're looking for a name, call me Nem."

"Do you know where my sister is?" I ask.

"No, but I can fill in some of the missing pieces you're looking for."

"What missing pieces?"

"I can tell you how they're using her to find you. Because everything that has happened to you these past days is because of how easily they can find you. Because they're not playing fair, so I'm here to balance the scale. Because you know how I called you a bringer of death? Frankly you're not very good at it. Because there are some things you need to learn over the coming days and there are few people left who can teach you. Because you're looking for one of those last few like yourself and to find her you're going to need to take in what I teach you quickly."

"Ok, but what's that got to do with my sister?" I ask.

"I'm getting there, I'm getting there. It would be too ironic to talk about how impatient you are. To understand who has your sister, you need a history lesson. It's going to be a long story so get comfortable. We need to go back to what started the veil war, since your generation seems to have lost all knowledge on what really happened. Here's what you need to know.

"The veil, as you call it, isn't just these realms of free flowing energy, as most of you humans seem to think. Roaming those energy planes are entities, some sentient, some not so. Some are simple; all they do is feed off of stray energy and each other. Like me, there are others far more intelligent. And they have various intentions behind their existence.

"In histories past, when they've decided to interact with humans, humans have called them many things: gods, demons, angels, spirits, familiars. The list goes on. None of those definitions captures their essence, but humans...."

"Gee thanks." I roll my eyes at her.

Nem ignores me and continues talking. "Before the veil war, the government was run by a circle of talented who, by the very exceptional nature of their abilities, were able to keep control of the population, as governments are wont to do. Those you call Nons, like your parents, were a separate faction, constantly persecuted by that government. I guess it was just for being different. There was a lot of fear about their potential.

"The Nons fought a losing battle. They were divided. A splinter sect was formed by those that were willing to go to any length to bring down the government. And of course, it only takes a few bad apples to ruin things for everyone. Those with malicious intent don't go looking for angels now do they?

"The government discovered this sect's plan and panicked, naturally. It turned from run of the mill persecution into a policy of outright elimination. And they saw no difference between Nons, believing any could be corrupted.

"For a long while, the Nons held out, despite the immense pressure upon them from the government. Your parents had a lot to do with that. Things were heading towards a stalemate. People were tiring of the war.

"To break the stalemate, the talented government of the time devised an ingenious plan to empower the non-psychic proletariat in an attempt to bring overwhelming numbers into the war. They developed a fanatical religious military force to hunt Nons. They patterned it on a bastardised memory of an army long forgotten, the Knights Templar. Of course, given the rather broad fanaticism that had been honed in their training, when the government let their dogs off their leash it didn't take long for them to turn on their masters. The hunters became the hunted.

"Those in the circle running the government quickly lost their heads, but the Templars were non-discriminant. If you were talented you were fair game. They established their own puppet government and set to work eliminating anybody with even the smallest amount of talent. The Nons, given their greater potential, were particularly targeted. The Templars were relentless to such an extent that there are few talented humans left to tell the true history of the war. The loss of lives and the large scale destruction during the second phase of the war was the greatest devastation humans have ever witnessed. Your generation doesn't have the remotest idea of what humanity lost to that destruction.

"Nobody ever talks about what the war was about," I say.

"Maybe they're ashamed? Who knows? Maybe you'll be able to find somebody to ask one day."

"So why are they suddenly targeting me? And how are they using my sister to do it?" I ask.

"As vicious as the Templar are, they've always been fairly one-tracked. Shoot first, ask questions later, you know? But now it's clear somebody else is pulling the strings. And that somebody has been trying to reach out to some of the most malicious of entities from across the veil. That's where you and your sister come into it. As Nons you have the unique ability to cross the veil. For years they've held her, looking for a way to use her as a conduit through the veil. Unwilling to push her too hard in case they damaged her, they've had little success. But these are the kinds of entities who have centuries of practice being patient.

"And then they captured you. With you, they now had somebody to experiment with, to push, to learn the best methods to twist your sister against her very nature."

"So me getting captured made things worse for my sister?" I ask.

"Very much so," Nem says. "As for how they're finding you, you and your sister share a bond, a permanent link between you. Most people who spend time together form some sort of bond. For your sister to have hidden it this long is impressive. She did well. But knowing the bond exists between you the government could easily tap it and trace that link to locate you.

"You have a choice to make and considering how long you've been sitting here, you need to make it quickly. Then you need to get the hell away from here."

I interrupt, "What choice?"

"Your choice is this," Nem continues. "We cut the link. Without it, whoever is watching you won't be able to use it as an anchor to find you. Once it's cut though it's cut for good. You'll lose that bond with your sister. The other option is to take a page from their book and trace the link in the other direction, to the location of your sister. Of course, without breaking the link, they're going to know exactly where you are, all the time. You'll be constantly on the run. How long do you think you can keep that up?"

"That's not a choice," I say frustrated. "Damned if I do, damned if I don't. And how are we going to do it anyway? How are they doing it?" I ask.

Cara stares at Nem. "Did you bring us together on purpose?"

She turns back to me and begins explaining, "Remote viewing. It's an ability that, to some extent, allows you to 'see' a place remotely. It's similar to my precognitive ability. But while my talent moves through time to show images, a viewer's ability lets them move spatially. They normally need an anchor though, something to locate themselves in space else it's hit and miss at best. Your link with your sister is perfect for that. While there are other talents that can be used for tracking someone, RV works the most consistently. As for knowing somebody able to do it, I know one." Cara pauses. "Though, she's going to be difficult to convince."

"Why, who is it?"

"Yeah..." She drags out the word, trying to avoid it, "I didn't say it was going to be easy to convince them to help though."

"It's her sister," Nem says.

"You have a sister?" I ask.

"Yeah, I have a sister. We don't really see eye to eye all that often." Cara says.

"Where is she?" I ask.

"We don't speak much. But I know where she'll be, assuming she's not out on a job: The Sedition Bar; a talent safehouse slash club on the south side of the city. The name is a play on the Resistance Bar. But it's, well.... While the Resistance Bar is – was – neutral ground and tended to attract those actually interested in helping the resistance the Sedition Bar on the other hand, while still considered neutral territory tends to attract the more extreme less legal elements of our society. Less welcoming. It's quite a long walk from where we are and I'm not sure how my sister will take seeing me again."

"Right at this moment you have more pressing concerns," Nem says. "I suggest you work that out somewhere else? If you don't move now you're going to have company."

"Again?" I exclaim.

"Yes well, you did make the choice not to break the link and it's not going to make life easy for you. You know you could always stay and fight?" she says.

I shake my head. "I think enough I've seen enough fighting for a while."

Nem just lets out a cackling laugh. "You haven't even started yet girl."

"Too late!" Cara yells. "Run!"

Across the field I can see soldiers with their telltale white armbands heading towards us. As they get close enough to recognise us, they suddenly pick up the pace, switching from a stalking pace to a flat out run towards us. I snap out of my reverie. Cara edges me to start running. I guess I shouldn't be told twice. Nem flies off my shoulder and into the sky. How helpful.

We bolt toward the trees, aiming for the nearest walking path. We hit it running. I hope Cara knows where she's going, though I have some serious doubts. It takes only a few strides along the path for the warm sun to disappear. And while the path is cold and damp, it's not unpleasant. The vegetation is thick and heavy, almost rainforest-like. In a better time I would have enjoyed coming here.

My indulgence in this moment is short-lived. We turn a corner on the path. Not far in front of us is an iron wrought fence, black and rust, held in place by solid brick pylons. It looks unclimbable, especially with two soldiers waiting for us on the other side. They're ready for us. What appeared to be an effective escape route is instead a rather well-laid trap.

The soldiers chasing us slow their pace to a walk; the trap is sprung and we have nowhere to go. Nem's final words seem more a lot more prophetic now. I guess we have only just started. We turn to face our pursuers.

Naive

As we reached the fence, I failed notice that Nem settled herself onto my shoulder. I'm not sure how one misses the addition of such a large bird upon one's shoulder, but her ability to arrive in silence scares me as much as the soldiers surrounding us. And although I can feel her there, she's entirely weightless. It's an unusual sensation.

"I hope you are not so naïve to consider yourself trapped. Or do I have to do everything myself?" She lets out an audible sigh. Perhaps I'm missing something, but naïvety seems like the least of my problems right now. They have both directions covered.

Then things get crazy. Nem launches herself with a single stroke of her wings. She morphs as she moves through the air, landing a dark human entity, the second I've seen in the last two days. She's different, definitely shorter than that first one, shorter than me, and with her more solid outline and long flowing hair, I'm sure she's not the entity met before. But how can one truly tell the difference between shades of black?

With such inhuman speed, she seems almost to flicker out of existence between two giant strides towards the closest soldier. Her hand reaches out and appears to grab him by the throat but to my surprise passes through him. As it leaves his body her hand drags energy, in human form, her fingers wrapped around its throat.

She pauses just a moment, shoulder to shoulder with him. The energy she holds dissipates quickly. He falls, dead.

She turns, deliberately, facing the next soldier. I blink. She stands behind him, her right arm draped over his shoulder and across his chest; a wicked embrace. Her eyes glow brighter. Shock spreads across his face as her black hand erupts through his chest. There's something disturbing about her posture that makes her appear to be smiling. He falls backwards, right through her incorporeal body. She did that far too easily.

"Get the girl out of here!" yells one of the men behind the fence.

I turn around to see the remaining soldiers grab hold of the girl, the same strange one there the day I was captured. Of all things, how curious it is that she is here. Perhaps she's the one they're using to track me? They move quickly, reacting to the deaths of the other soldiers and drag her into an awaiting van before Nem can get to them. It seems even Nem has her limits. The door on the van slams shut as it goes screeching off.

"Damn, oh well," Nem says nonchalantly.

"Having fun down there, Sister?" a voice calls from high in the trees above us. To my surprise, another entity, distinctly feminine in silhouette and as completely black and featureless as Nem, sits on a branch above us. Her legs swing freely, playfully, like she doesn't have to worry about falling from of the tree. From here it looks like she's having fun. Or maybe she's just delighted by the killing. Should I be more disturbed? I find myself unmoved, as if this is just a standard part of my life now.

"Why hello up there, Machie, how is my older sister?" Nem calls out.

"You know I hate it when you call me that," she replies, her inflection implying bemusement rather than real annoyance. "And I'm going to need to leave." She looks into the distance. "I can't leave her for too long, she's still strong, but nothing lasts forever."

She pushes herself off the branch, morphing into a crow as she falls. With a flap of wings she's gone.

"Stay safe big sister," Nem says with the softest of whispers.

She faces me, takes one quick step and jumps morphing back into her crow form to land upon my shoulder. "You know, you look like you've seen a ghost," she says into my ear.

"You turned into a human," I say, still trying to comprehend everything that just happened.

She tilts her head at me, suggesting my statement seems unusual. "It happens. Just don't ask me to become a cow," she humours.

After a short pause, her voice turns inquisitive, asking, "You've seen someone like us before, haven't you? I can see it on your face."

I nod. "She was just like you and yet I could tell you are different. But it's not exactly easy to tell. It wasn't you then, was it?"

"No, it wasn't me," Nem says. "When did you see her?"

"She helped me escape from the Templars."

Nem snorts. "Hah! And here I was thinking you managed that by yourself. It wasn't me," she says. "And I don't know who it was. Now you've gone and made me curious. I was sure you didn't get any help and it's not like me to miss the presence of another. And that is very curious indeed."

"What the fuck just happened?" Cara asks, interrupting.

"Were you not paying attention dear?" Nem replies. "Death just happened. Now they know where you are, which means you need to be somewhere else, very quickly."

"Come on. Let's get the hell out of here then," I say, stepping up to the fence to size it up. "Hey hold up. When you chose to lead us down this path, how the hell did you expect us to get over this fence?" I ask.

The cast iron fence is a lot higher than I noticed before and from my current point of view it doesn't seem particularly climbable. The top is topped with pointed bars and it is far too tall to vault while the brick support posts seem also too tall to provide an alternative place to climb over. Cara responds to my question by reaching up and grabbing the brick lip near the top of one of the brick support posts, lifting a foot onto the iron cross-beam and gracefully launching herself over in one sweeping motion. She makes it look easy.

"Right," I say in awe.

My efforts are far less graceful. After scraping my forearm painfully on the bricks I stretch my leg up onto the top of fence. Without these gloves this would have been far more painful. As I try to vault over I catch my foot on one of the points on the top. Instead of Cara's graceful motion I tumble head first over the top and landing hard on my back.

I spend the next moments recovering from having the wind knocked out of me. I struggle to get my breath. And I can tell I'm going to have a nice lump on the back of my head. Cara just stands there and laughs at me. I really don't see the humour in it. As if to rub it in, Nem joins in with her laughter, perched on the top of fence.

"Gee thanks," I say, standing myself up. "You could have at least helped me up."

Cara, ignoring my glare, responds with another outburst of laughter, struggling to keep herself upright.

"Come on, come on, you've got to move on. They'll be back here shortly with more reinforcements," Nem says.

"Do you know how to get from here to where you said your sister is?" I ask Cara.

"Sure," Cara says, "though I'm not sure an impossibly black bird with glowing red eyes is inconspicuous enough for where we're going. Nem, you're going to need to avoid being seen if we're going to walk amongst the public."

"I can keep an eye on you from above," Nem says. With a flap of wings she launches off my shoulder.

You know, having a crow, especially a talking one that claims to be an honest to goodness harbinger of death, circle above us is rather off-putting. It's fair to say that I'd dodged Death's scythe a little too often these past few days. How much longer before the omen becomes my own?

◆

It's been a long day already and yet, I know it's only just begun. The most important thing at the moment though? I'm so hungry.

"Do you think you might know somewhere with some food around here?" I ask.

"Sure, there should be something around here," Cara responds. "Think you'll be ok here for a moment? I think it's better if I go get food by myself and bring it back."

This doesn't sound like the best of ideas to me.

"You sure?" I ask. "You will be back?"

She smiles convincingly at me. "Yes, of course I will, but in the short time I've known you, you have this habit of making a scene whenever you're in public. It's probably best we avoid any more scenes for a while."

The truth is worth a laugh. "Ok."

I sit down on some stairs at the entrance of a building and watch her walk off. I hope she's coming back.

♦

Cara returns, handing me a paper-wrapped bread roll. The chicken and salad roll it contains looks delicious. Now that the adrenaline has worn off though, the food is depressingly tasteless. Not tasteless enough to leave the tomato in, though. It has to go. It's been forever since I had real chicken; it's impossible to find in the outer suburbs. Unless it's stolen, which I'm fairly confident it was, the last time I ate it.

We walk through the city, eating our respective lunches quietly.

"How far away are you taking me?" I ask, between bites.

"It should be about an hour's walk from here, if we do it quickly," she says.

Will we even last an hour before they catch up to us? Should we be worried they'll work out where we're going? This morning they seemed to be getting quicker at finding us. The thought just depresses me further.

Cara picks up on my mood, and, breaking the silence, asks, "You worried?"

"Yeah," I respond. The curt response is not the friendliest of answers. She's not to blame.

"What if they work out where we're heading?" I ask.

"We'll just need to keep moving and avoid obvious landmarks so that they don't. Hopefully, that will be enough to cover our tracks."

"And even if your sister can find my sister, how do we get her out?" I ask.

She shakes her head at me, concerned. "I have no idea. We just have to work that out when the time comes."

"Do you really believe that?"

She stares into the distance. "Yesterday I believed I was absolutely safe with the resistance. Not sure I can believe anything anymore." She sighs. "I'm sorry I don't have a better answer for you." She takes my hand and softly squeezes. "I guess we will just have to work something out."

She doesn't let go.

♦

The rest of the city is passed in silence. The city itself is dull, more than expected; we're in the inner circle of the city, but under the surface it is just as dirty and dreary as the outer suburbs I'm used to. On the surface everything appears better, the buildings, the people, the food. But underneath it's no different. With so few people on the streets, it appears just as abandoned. What do these people do all day?

We go out of our way to avoid passing too closely to the few people with whom we cross paths. Too far out of the way I think. I wonder if it makes us stand out more. Frankly though, no-one seems interested in us. Is it undue paranoia? Perhaps.

"How do you know if this place will be open when we get there?" I ask, to break the silence.

She laughs at that. "Of course it will be," she says. "This is the kind of place that never closes."

We fall silent again. I've never been good at small talk, but as we walk through this dull place I struggle to start even the most basic of conversations with Cara. What is there to talk about? *Hi, how are you? Sorry about your dead friends. Weather is pretty good isn't it? How do you feel about holding hands with a violent psychic killer?*

Here I am, staring at the most beautiful woman I've met, somebody who instantly befriended me despite everything I am, somebody who's been dragged through hell because of who I am, and I can't manage a simple conversation with her. Why?

She seems to pick up on me staring at her, though her choice of topic is perhaps the one thing I didn't want to think about.

"Tell me about your friend Aine. What was she like? Were you two...?" She leaves the question open.

Were we what? *Oh.* She couldn't have picked a worse way to break the tension.

Panic spreads across Cara's face. "You don't have to talk about it if you don't want to."

I shake my head with a sympathetic smile. "No, it's ok. And no, we weren't. I've never really had anybody like that in my life. Where we're from, there wasn't exactly a plethora of people with which to develop relationships. Certainly nobody who seemed interested in sullen old me. No, she was... I don't know." Fifteen years and I struggle to think of a single word to describe her. "Strong willed. She was a kine; you know what they're like. But she was sweet in her own way, a good friend, my only one really. I mean, we didn't have anybody else growing up; it was just the two of us against the world. We never really found any purpose. We didn't have anybody else. She was younger than me, though I don't remember us ever not being friends. We explored the outer limits; the derelict buildings and abandoned parks. Most of the time it was me listening, while she did all the talking. She wasn't much of a philosopher, but she always had something to talk about." I laugh at that thought. "She was a lot more focused on what was going on around her. I think now that I should have paid more attention to what she had to say. I certainly could have taken a leaf out of her book more often than I did.

"Then that day they just came and shot her. Bang, all over. As if she was nothing. She meant something to me, so why take me? Why take me and not her? I don't feel special."

Why was I ok with talking about this? I keep thinking about that day, replaying the motions of the cops. Or were they soldiers? I can't remember.

What I need is to change the subject. "Tell me about your sister. Were you close?" I ask.

Oh well done me, that's a *perfect* change of subject. As if you couldn't make this situation more awkward you had to drop that question. And judging by her facial expression, she's thinking the same. She snaps out of it though and nods her head at me.

"Yeah, we were close once. We're twins," she says, unexpectedly. "When we were younger were inseparable. You know, matching clothes, finishing each other's sentences, all that kind of stuff. Then we both ended up on the wrong side of town, I guess. Without any family but each other we didn't really have any direction.

"We were about sixteen when we found out that our talents were highly desirable in the less than legal psychic community, particularly in the employ of thieves. We got involved with one particular group that raided the houses of people known to be important to the government and other well-to-do members of the city. She'd use her remote viewing to locate valuables in buildings and draw maps for the heists, while I acted as a preternatural look-out during the heists. But before long we weren't just helping them plan robberies any more, we were in there, participating. I guess at the time the thrill of it sucked us in, but I don't know now. We were young. You understand.

"But the group was falling apart from the start; infighting lead to schism and people started to peel away, start their own groups and plan their own jobs. Caitlin wanted us to stretch out on our own as well. But I think even then I knew that that life couldn't last forever. Feuds had become personal, violent at times. I wanted out. After that, we just drifted apart. The resistance came to me looking to use my skills. I tried to get her to join me but I think now she's too far in to get out."

The pain of those events is displayed on Cara's face. Why help me chase a sister who I've never met, at a great risk to herself, when she could be working on her relationship with her own sister?

The conversation drifts off, thankfully, to more mundane subjects, mostly revolving around how neither of us is used to this much exercise in a day. The city itself passes by uneventfully. You know, it seems like once upon a time it may have been beautiful; as beautiful as any city, I suppose. The further we travel from the inner city and towards the outer skirts the more obvious the impact of the war. Each city block takes me closer to a more familiar world. The sun paints fire through the sky and with the scars of war illuminated all around me it's hard not to feel like I'm once again walking into hell.

With Arms Wide Open

The sun dips below the horizon and the temperature falls with it.

"We're almost there," Cara says. "I'm not looking forward to going back. It's been such a long time. I should warn you, they're not particularly accepting of strangers. Don't expect a welcome mat rolled out for you."

We walk down a street full of neon and nightclubs; most just beginning to open their doors. The streets are already filled with people looking to get into these clubs. More people than I'd ever seen in the one place. Is this what people in the inner city do? None of the clubs seem particularly inviting to me though, frankly and I'm having some serious second thoughts about where I'm being taken.

We seem to be attracting a lot of attention. The gawkers are making me feel uncomfortable. It's pretty easy to feel like everyone is staring at you when all you want to do is disappear and disappear is what I want to be doing right now. Why are they staring so intently at us?

"Keep your eyes open and try not to stand out. There's something not right here. I can't tell what it is; it's being masked. Try to avoid drawing attention to yourselves," Nem says to me telepathically, her voice resonating weirdly through my mind, making me pause for a moment. It's not what I want to hear as I walk into the unknown.

Cara pulls me along, oblivious to the attention. "Come on, it's at the end of this street," she says.

The places along this street keep getting seedier and seedier the further we walk. Eventually the street runs out of clubs.

"Where is this place?" I ask.

She points down a side street, where two large men stand sentinel before a massive steel door.

"Hmmm, new guard, this might be a problem," she says with concern as she walks up to them.

"We need in," she says stiffly to the guard.

"And who the hell are you? The clubs are back that way, down the street." He motions with his head. "Fuck off."

At that moment the big steel door opens and a man sticks his head out. "Calm the fuck down there," he says to the bouncer. Well, would you look at what the cat dragged in?" He says unimpressed, at Cara.

"She's one of us," he says, turning back to the doorman. "Or at least she used to be. She'll behave. Won't she?" He turns away before Cara can answer.

The guard reluctantly steps out of the way, letting us slip through the heavy door. Inside a grinding tempo of heavy bass notes reverberates down the hallway.

"Sorry about that, these new guards aren't the most switched on and I got held up," The man says. "Now..." He turns quickly to Cara and roughly pushes her against the hallway wall. "What the fuck are you doing here and what the fuck was going through your head when you decided to bring her here?"

Cara doesn't blink, firing back an aggressive retort. "It's good to see you too, Calix. Where's my fucking sister?"

"Oh, she is going to be thrilled to see you," he says. "Everyone will be when they see her. What the fuck is going through your head? That fucking government-issue langseax on her belt isn't exactly inconspicuous."

My hand self-consciously reaches for my belt. So that's what all the stares were for. I'd forgotten I was wearing it. So much for being less conspicuous.

"There are people here who'd be more than willing to slit her throat just for carrying that. But worse, it's well known that she's being tracked and yet you knowingly brought her here. Are you insane?"

I really don't like this talking about me as if I'm not here thing. And if he doesn't let go of Cara I'm willing to pull the damn knife and force the issue. He backs off and keeps walking, thankfully.

"Word has spread of the attention your friend here seems to attract and there are lot of people here who suspect she's a government plant. Try not to get yourself killed," he says. "You'll find sister is where she usually is."

Already the few people standing around in this entrance hallway have taken an interest in us. A few don't appear to be entirely lucid at the moment. Some seem curious. Others still are showing signs of open hostility towards us. Those appear to be the most dangerous looking of the lot.

We quicken our pace to pass them. The hallway opens into a large high-ceilinged room filled with fluorescent cyan lights and multi-coloured lasers pulsing in time to dark electronic music. A dance floor packed with people occupies the majority of the space. Surrounding the dance floor, stages hold dancing women; most scantily clad, some even less, all swaying to the beat of the music. Next to those stages and around the edges of the room reclining upon couches are groups of people in varied levels of animation. There are a few heated conversations going on though it's impossible to hear what is being argued over the volume of the music. Across from the dance floor is a free standing bar around which a few people are seated on stools, seemingly paying attention to only their drinks. The bar and dance stages visually reflect the building's previous industrial history; repurposed piping and steel panels, all in various stages of rusting. The room has kept its cold concrete floor and, despite the light show, the inadequate lighting fails to illuminate the corners beyond twisting shadows.

It's from those shadows that most of the attention is directed at us. Heads turn to stare at us as Calix leads us across the room. I swear it seems like some of their eyes are glowing in the darkness. Word spreads of our arrival like a ripple. By the time we reach our apparent destination, it feels like we have the undivided attention of everyone in building. Even the dancers have slowed to watch us. Some people start moving to leave. The atmosphere in the place chills.

My skin crawls, like dozens of people are caressing me all over. Thinking on some of the things I've learnt this past day, it's easy to suspect that some of them are. The thought of it sparks a fire of aggression that swells through me against such a violation. I'm ready to lash out.

"Come on, before you hurt yourself. They're waiting for you. You are totally unprepared for a place like this," Calix says, looking at me.

The feeling stops suddenly, snapping me back to reality with a shiver that runs through me. Calix laughs derisively at me. In a shadowy corner sit a small group of three, occupying a set of couches set up in a u-shape around a coffee table upon which sit the remains of a few drinks. They watch us intently as we're lead to them.

Only as we get close does Cara's sister become identifiable among them, sitting on the left. Despite the blunt, more aggressive cut of her bangs, the resemblance is obvious. Her expression makes her seem genuinely curious about our presence. If anything, she seems happy to see her sister. Cara stands back, reluctant to step closer.

Calix takes a seat on the right. Pushing past us, a younger man returns to take up a seat next to him, bringing with him a round of drinks. His outward appearance is messy, unkempt; his motion's erratic and fidgety. He takes up one of the drinks and hides behind it.

In the centre seat is a man, slightly older than the rest. While the others are wearing functional clothing, his is clean cut and expensive. Everyone in the group defers to him. While he sits back with relaxed authority, his face is nothing but hatred. From that I can tell this isn't going to go well.

Standing to his left is a young woman not much older than me, with long flowing blonde hair and steel blue eyes set to cut right through you. Currently they're staring directly through me. While Cara's sister shows curiosity and the man in control shows hatred, it's impossible to read the expression on her face. It also wouldn't surprise me in the slightest if she's turns out to be a kine. And judging by the way where she stands behind the man, she's probably his bodyguard.

"This is Logan." Cara starts introducing, beginning with the man in the centre.

The man, Logan, cuts her short, speaking with venom in his voice. "Cara, I cannot believe that you of all people would be stupid enough to bring her here," he says. "Word spread pretty quickly about the girl who brings down death upon every place she visits. What the fuck was going through your head when you thought to bring her, who is quite obviously being actively tracked by the Templars, into the single biggest underground psychic establishment in this city? Those same Templars which have decided lately to actively start hunting us down again."

You know, I'm starting to get sick of being spoken about as if I'm not here. I turn to Caitlin directly, distinctly turning away from him. "I need your help. I'm told that the people tracking me are doing so through a bond with my sister and that they're using remote viewing to find us. I need to find her. Your sister tells me that you'd be able to do something similar and track her down. Can you help me?"

Logan answers instead, scowling, "holy shit she is crazy." He talks past me to Cara. "I *will not* have members of my team running off getting themselves killed by the damn Templars just to help her with some fool's errand."

He looks at me and says matter of factly. "You say your sister was captured by the government? She's already dead. Get over it. You want to go chasing ghosts? Go find yourself a witch."

A witch? The insult cuts. But I need his help.

"But if they're still tracking me, she must still be alive."

He ignores me, turning back to Cara. "I don't know who she is and I don't give a shit. Get her the fuck out of here before she gets us all killed. Or I'll kill her myself."

That's enough of being referred to as if I am invisible. I'm tired, it's been a long day and I'm not going to let this stuck up bastard stop me from finding my sister. That aggressive feeling builds again. I'm not looking to stop it this time. I reach down to my belt as I take a couple of steps forward. Adrenaline preempts any need for a plan on how I can force him help me.

The bodyguard steps directly in front of me before I'm able to get much closer. She's imposes herself right on top of me, getting right up in my face while putting a firm hand on my shoulder. It's then she does the unexpected. She leans down and whispers into my ear, a soft and gentle voice. "Not like this. He's nothing. This will just get you killed. There will be other ways."

The lack of edge to her voice disarms me, though she keeps a firm hand on my shoulder. Over her shoulder Caitlin looks despondently up at me. "I'm sorry." She says to me. She shrugs with a pained look on her face. I guess Cara was right; she is lost to this world.

The bodyguard turns her head to face their leader. "I'll lead them out and make sure that they make it."

"Yes, please do," he says, frustrated, waving us away.

"Come on, this way." she says, pushing me ahead of her.

"So what do we do now?" I ask Cara as we walk away.

"I'm not sure," she says. "Perhaps we'll find somebody else able to help us. I'm sure that there must be others. We'll just have to keep asking around at other places, there are other places we can go to."

The crowd parts for us as we walk back towards the entrance again. We walked all this way, to be turned away so easily? I feel lost. What am I supposed to do now? It's difficult to think clearly, I can feel how tired I am.

Cara steps out onto the street first, quickly taking a few steps to distance herself from the place. I'm slower, my pace limited by the weight of my thoughts. As soon as I step out though I can tell straight away that something isn't right. Something is missing.

The sound of Nem's voice comes screaming into my head. "Get out of there!" Where the hell is she?

Then I realise. The door guard is missing. There's movement in the corner of my eye. A new black van parked a few metres down the street is open.

"Oh no."

The Lights Only Hide the Darkness

I scream out to Cara. Too slowly. Far too slowly. Soldiers seize her before she can react. They drag her into a waiting van, even as more soldiers move towards me.

A firm set of arms pull me back through the club doorway. The woman, the bodyguard, holds me steady. I fight to free myself from her, but she's far too strong. The steel door slams shut, stopping the soldiers from getting to me. And preventing me from getting to Cara. On the back of the door a large steel rod slides across though no hand moves it, locking the door.

Cara... I fight to get free. I can't let them take her.

"Calm down, calm down," the firm voice of the arms that hold me says. "There's nothing you can do about it now. We have to get you and everybody else out of here."

Already, people in the club are panicking, looking to get out. Word spread quickly of what happened outside. I'm pulled firmly back, deeper into the club.

"What do we do? Are we trapped in here?" I ask, scared. Right now, I couldn't feel more alone.

"You don't think a den of thieves would have a few escape routes available?" She says, guiding me through the chaos and towards the bar. Everyone else appears to be trying to head in the other direction. As we push past the crowd a hand reaches out and grabs me by the wrist, holding me firmly. A hood covers the man's head making it difficult to see who is holding me.

The lights shifts momentarily and I get a flash of a middle aged man with greying hair and a longish beard. I reach for my knife as panic sets in. The room dims as time freezes.

"You are a long way from home, Nem," he says looking past me.

I feel a wave of heat spread through my head and it feels like my sinuses are about to explode.

My lips move, out of my control. A voice, my own, responds to him, "We both are."

"Will you watch over mine as you look over your own?" he says.

"There will be no songs sung for her any time soon. Thank you," my voice says.

He lifts is head up to look at me. Although it's difficult to see his face under the hood I can see that the right side of his face is heavily bandaged. One eye stares through me.

"And to you little one, while I cannot help you find your sister, but I can offer you this: Do not think that you are alone in your fight. Forces are aligning to even the balance even as those who work against you seek to grow their power."

He tilts his head to look past me at my guardian. "Take care of her, Allison. And deal with that fool you've been working with before he hurts somebody."

"Of course," she responds with a cocky chuckle. She takes me by the arm. "Come on, we need to get out of here."

Light comes rushing back into the room as time unfreezes. The man disappears, in a blink, as if he was never there. What the hell? Something just happened here and I don't have a clue what it was.

"Sorry about taking over like that," Nem says, her voice reverberating through my head. "It would appear that you've just gained a very powerful ally."

"How did he disappear like that? He was just here..." I ask confused.

Nem answers, "What makes you think he was ever here?"

"Come on," Allison says, with more urgency, "we really need to get out of here."

She pushes me towards a door behind the bar area. It seems to be the least busy of the exits people are trying to squeeze through.

Caitlin runs up to us, screaming, "Where's my sister?"

She stands in front of me, eyes red, violently shaking me while screaming it again and again.

Logan follows casually behind her. He looks at me in disgust and says, "You should be thankful I don't have you killed for this. Caitlin, Allison, leave her before she gets us all killed. We need to get out of this place."

Allison steps towards him. Her fist hits him in the face with a resounding crack; he collapses to the floor, on one knee stunned. "Be thankful I don't just kill you now." She says, coldly.

Blood flows willingly from his nose. His attempt to stand up is shaky at best.

"You've just signed your own death warrant for that," he spits from his knees.

Allison holds a hand, palm out towards him and with a telekinetically charged thump of air, pushes him over again.

"Stop!" The man cries out, struggling to his hands and knees again.

Allison scowls in disgust, then takes another step towards him and kicks him in the ribs, hard. The sound echoes through the now emptying room. He curls up on the floor, winded.

"Do you think you'll be able to track your sister?" She asks Caitlin.

She nods her head rapidly in affirmation, eyes wide. "I didn't think of that."

"Then let's get out of here already." Allison says impatiently.

"Where can we go?" I ask.

"Follow me," Caitlin says impassively.

◆

"Welcome to my place." Caitlin says flatly as she types a security code into the door of the apartment she's lead us to.

"Are you crazy?" I ask. "Why have you taken us to your place? This security won't stop them. What if they track me here?"

"They won't."

"How do you know that?"

"They won't."

I lost count of the number of different security measures needed to get in this apartment complex has Caitlin led us to. I hope that's not what she's relying on, because I can't see that stopping the Templars.

Caitlin turns on the lights to reveal a warm apartment, small, but filled luxuriously. She and her sister share similar tastes. Dozens of landscape sketches adorn the walls. Despite the warmth the house portraits, the place appears untouched and unlived in.

"Make yourselves at home while I find a map and some paper." Caitlin yells as she goes searching in another room. "Damn it, I can't seem to find out any paper."

"The door opens, go out on balcony if you want," Caitlin calls out before returning to her search. This may take some time."

Sliding the glass door open, I step outside; the air is cold, too cold for comfort, yet somehow suitable. Leaning out over the balcony is a new experience for me. I've never been this high up before. The city is spread before me, a foreign landscape still brightly lit at this hour.

Allison joins me; she leans against the balcony next to me, silent, waiting patiently, her face unreadable as she looks out over the city. But I can't find the words to begin talking to her. I don't understand why she would follow me. Why she would risk helping me.

"We'll find her," Allison eventually says.

"How do you know?" I ask.

"No matter what it takes, I will help you find her."

"Why? Why are you helping me?" I ask.

"You're not the only person to have lost family to the government." A momentary flash of anger crosses her face. Up until now she had been completely detached.

"I was thirteen when a patrol of Templars caught my brother and me. He was sixteen. One of the soldiers held a knife to my throat while another raped me. They forced my brother to watch while they took turns. Then, once they were sated, they turned to him and shot him. I still remember his face, the look of shock as his blood poured through his hands.

"Until then, I thought I wasn't talented. My brother was a kine, just like my mother and father. I thought I was the odd one out; thirteen years old and no hint of any telekinetic talent. That changed that night. I killed them both. With telekinesis I pushed the knife away from my throat. Tore it from his grip. And I stabbed it into them, again and again, until exhaustion finally overwhelmed my fury.

"It was my Master who found me that night, crying next to my brother's lifeless body. He took me in and he helped me focus. He gave me purpose. I owe him everything. All he asks in return is that I always keep fighting. Never give up. Because you don't know what fate has in store. You can't change what will happen, only stare it down resolutely."

"But all of you are risking so much helping me. Who am I to you? I'm just some random stranger; a nobody. I mean nothing to you. I don't want more people to get hurt because of me. It might be best if I just give myself up. Organise a trade with the Templars, her for me.

"Don't be stupid, I would never give up one of us to the government. Never." She stresses never with bitter surety. "I can't let them hurt her."

"You really care about her, don't you?"

I keep silent for a moment. "I'm just tired of running."

"We'll find her, and when we do, there'll be no more running," Allison says. "Come back inside. Rest while you can. You look like you need it. "

She guides me inside and sits me down on Caitlin's scarlet couch. I curl up in the corner while they organise themselves.

Reunion

"Wake up, wake up". Somebody is shaking my shoulder. Eyes open. Night still hangs on outside. I must have fallen asleep. Allison is the one trying to wake me. Caitlin stands over a large kitchen table covered in sketches.

"How long was I asleep?" I ask. Not long enough... I feel wrecked. Sleep still has her grasp firmly on my consciousness.

Allison answers. "Two hours or so, maybe three. We didn't have the heart to wake you."

Two hours? My heart drops. We've got to get out of here.

"How the hell have we managed to stay in one place for two hours? I ask in a panic. "We've got to leave, now! They'll find us here!"

"You know, you panic too quickly." Caitlin answers with a scowl. "Don't you think, as an RV'er, that I wouldn't have some sort of defences against it? I've taken steps to prevent others from RV'ing into here. It should keep them busy for a while."

I look at her confused. "What steps? How can you not be panicking?"

"The walls are all shielded. Anybody walking in here disappears. I assumed that the people tracking you are using you as an anchor. This room blocks any link they might use to track you. In here you vanish into a psychic void. And that's not the only trick this place has. It also obscures its own location. Anyone that looks too closely is likely to go on a wild goose chase to try and untangle things. It should keep them guessing for a while."

"Wait, did you say it'll break the link? What about my sister," I say in a panic. "You mean I've lost the link to my sister? I can't lose that, that's all I have to find her."

"It just blocks people looking in. Once we step out, it should be fine again."

"Should?"

"Settle down already," Allison says. "Besides, we have more news on that as well."

Caitlin continues, "Yeah, we started off tracking Cara, which has been really difficult since they were moving her by vehicle. That made it really hard to get a solid anchor so I struggled to get a decent image. By the time I got a solid picture, they had stopped for the night at some sort of hotel, toward the western outer suburbs that we've located on the map and, from that, Allison thinks she knows where they intend to take her. Given how close they are to their likely destination, we are, however, confused why they didn't just keep going.

"And you have news about my sister? You've managed to track her down?" I ask, excited.

They all nod at me, solemn expressions matching.

"What, what's wrong?"

"Don't get too hopeful," Caitlin says. "We're pretty sure we know where they're keeping her. And it's the same place we think they're taking Cara. Are you familiar with Le Castel Blanc?"

I shake my head.

"Ok, so you know where the Viridis River divides the city and where the Viridian Woods grows along either side?

"Of course, though I've only seen the outer suburb side," I respond.

"Well, secluded within the Viridian Woods, on the inner side, the Templars constructed their high command centre, Le Castel Blanc. The place is a damn fortress, it's a modern castle. We're better off getting my sister back before they take her there. It'll be much easier to hit her captors before that get to that compound, but we'll need to do it quickly."

"And how do we do that?" I ask, wondering how us three are going to manage that.

"We get help," Allison says. "Once she's safe, we can work out how to get your sister out."

Will they even help me once we've gotten Cara back? I stand up and walk across to the table. Some of the sketches in front of Caitlin show different up-close images of a massive stone or perhaps concrete fortress, a modern take on castle. Some of the sketches show the castle from a distance in its surrounds, the thick grove of evergreen pine trees that make up the Viridian Woods, while others still focus in on the soldiers guarding the walls with automatic rifles.

It doesn't look like the sort of place you'd just walk up to and ask to be let in. Though what did I expect really?

"That place looks impenetrable. How the hell do we get in there?"

Nem picks that moment to fly in through the glass wall. She morphs as she flies through the air until she settles sitting on the edge of the table as a human, hands holding on to the edge and with feet swinging merrily, like a child.

"Oh, that's simple. You walk in through the front door," she says. You can almost see her smug smile.

Allison and Caitlin look at her incredulously.

"That sounds as far from simple as it gets. Caitlin's pictures show them armed. And I'm sure they'll be quite willing to point those guns at us if we try walking in through the front door." I say cynically. "You're kidding, right?"

"I don't know why you doubt yourself so much. You'd be perfectly capable of doing it if you bothered to think about it a little," Nem says. "If you're smart, you might consider not killing those holding Cara captive, perhaps gain some valuable information. Maybe even score yourselves a few uniforms, hmm?"

With eyes open in wonder, Caitlin's first thoughts of the situation are succinct. "I'm not even going to ask; at least she speaks the truth."

Nem climbs onto the tabletop and clambers, on hands and knees, over to the map. "So show me on the map where they're holding Cara."

Caitlin points. "It's this building. We think it must be some sort of government-run hotel or holding house or something."

Nem shifts back to her crow form on the table, and hops to the edge. "Ok, I'm going to go check it out. It shouldn't take long to get there, as the crow flies." And leaving us with that corny joke, she flies off through the glass wall.

"Ok, please tell me what the hell that was!" Caitlin exclaims.

"Who the hell was that, is the more correct question. That was Nem. And if she hears you call her a 'what' she's liable to kill you."

Allison takes a step back from the table. "I'm heading out to get us some help. We're going to need it if we're going to pull this off. I'll be back in no more than an hour. If I'm not back by then, get out of here." She walks across to me and looks me in the eyes. "You'll be ok. If we're going to do this, we're going to need help. I don't expect any problems, but if there are, just get out of here. While you wait for Nem to come back we could do with a bit more information on what we're getting into. Try and find out anything else you can about the people holding Cara."

She walks quickly from the room, leaving me wondering what to do now.

Caitlin seems intent on whatever it is that she's doing, unconcerned with Allison leaving. Lifting a pencil up, her brow goes taut in concentration while her eyes stare through the paper in front of her. She shakes her head and looks at me, worry filling her face. Worry turns to frustration as she slams the pencil against the table. Half of the snapped pencil rolls towards me.

"Why am I having so much trouble seeing this?"

"What's wrong?" I ask.

"I just can't seem to get a clear picture. I've never have this much of an issue. Everything is blurry." She shakes her head.

"You're worried about your sister," I try to reassure her, wrapping an arm around her shoulders. "It's little wonder you're having trouble concentrating."

"Maybe," she responds, unconvinced.

The silence that follows is awkward. Not that there's anything I can really do to help her. It's an awkward walk back to the couch, trying to avoid looking too useless. I stare up at the night sky, thinking of nothing else but Cara; the stars offer no suggestions. Night, the black void, absorbs all my thoughts.

Or maybe not. I bounce back to the table excited. "Are you able to explain to me how you do it?" I ask her. "Maybe I can help?"

She gives me a look that shows very clearly I should stop annoying her and she doesn't believe me. Regardless, she's polite enough to explain it to me anyway.

"I really don't know how to explain it very well. I just think of the person or object and a link seems to form between us. It helps a lot if I know roughly where the objects or person is because then in my head I can

116

guide the link as it forms. If I follow that link in my mind by, I don't know, projecting myself out, pictures will flash into my head, showing me things as if I were hovering over that object. I've learnt to hold those pictures in my mind long enough to sketch them. It's hard to keep steady, but I've learnt to control my position a little so I can get closer or further away and see more of the surroundings. Hopefully, from those images I'll be able to recognise a location or be able to sketch a decent map of the building," she patiently explains to me.

"When I was taught about using my abilities, there was a point where I needed to..." my face twists up as I struggle for the right words, "I don't know, push the image in my head from imaginary into reality. Is there the same thing with you?"

"Yeah definitely," she nods to me. "It's at the point when I project myself out. Hah. That's weird; I've never thought about it before, it just happens."

The thought must have helped because after a quick smile in acknowledgement she sets herself back to sketching with new fervour. At least I can bring a smile to her face.

Pencil in hand, I can do this. Forget the fact that you can't draw for shit. Eyes closed. Concentrate on Cara. Picture the bond form between us. Ok, now push out with my mind.

The next moments are a rush. How can I describe it? It feels like I'm floating, yet moving at a speed of hundreds of kilometres an hour. Such an amazing feeling. The earth rushes up to meet me, the world becoming clearer and clearer as an image of a place forms in my mind.

For a moment everything becomes clear. Cara stares directly back at me, almost as if she can see me. I see her kneeling in the center of the room with hands tied behind her back. She looks so scared.

Then it goes horrible wrong. My vision turns bright white as heavy static fills my ears. Then the pain comes. I bang my head against the table as the pain cuts me in half. The pain of hitting my head doesn't even register against the fire of every nerve in my brain burning from the inside out.

"Break the connection! Break the damn connection!"

Everything turns black.

♦

I come to, as somebody shakes me a little too vigorously for the massive headache I now have. "Hey, wake up, wake up." I open my eyes to a worried-looking Caitlin hovering over me. Somebody has moved me to the couch.

"What happened?" I ask.

"I don't know," Caitlin says, "You were standing over the table, then you fell suddenly, whacked your head on the table and passed out. You seemed ok, so I moved you to the couch to recover. What happened?"

"I really don't know. I saw Cara, briefly, for just a second. Then everything started hurting."

"You saw her?" Caitlin asks excitedly. "Tell me what you saw,"

"Didn't you?" I ask. Surely she was able to see her when she was viewing herself.

The look she gives me says otherwise. "No, I wasn't able to. Like I said, it was all blurry. No matter how hard I tried, I just couldn't focus."

Allison walks across to me. "Welcome back to the world of the living. You were out for quite a while. I brought help."

With a firm grip on my arm, she pulls me up. For the second time today I find myself in standing in front of Erik. He looks less than impressed.

"When Allison insisted on my help but wouldn't tell me for what, I had to know that somehow you were going to be involved.

Allison gives him a friendly push. "And yet you're still here. Be honest, the more fucked the situation, the more you enjoy it."

Erik grabs the map while slipping her a sly smile. "If what you say is true, then they must have had some sort of protection around her. Shit, if you've tripped something, they've probably worked out that we know where they are. We need to move now if we're to have any chance of catching them. Grab whatever else you think might help. Did you see how many of them there were?"

"No, I didn't see any actually. It happened so quickly that I'm struggling to remember what I did see. The place wasn't very big though. There couldn't have been more than a couple in there."

"Hmm, it sounds a little too easy. I guess we'll just have to wing it and hope there isn't more. Just to make sure, this motel that they're at, it's single storey yes?" he asks. "We want to avoid contact with the public if at all possible, obviously."

"Speaking of contact, has Nem been back?" I ask. "She should have returned by now."

"She's able to find you, right? Hopefully she's able to catch up to us."

"I'm not sure. I guess so. I'd rather not leave without her though."

Allison twists her face up, irritated. "We don't have time to wait for her. What about you Caitlin? I know this kind of stuff isn't really your thing."

"Are you kidding? I need to be there for my sister. There's no way in hell you're leaving without me." She says.

Erik cuts in before Allison can argue against it. "Whatever, this is wasting time. We really need to go folks."

He leads us down more stairs than I remember there being when we came. Geez I really must have been tired when we got here. Waiting for us in the building car park is, what is becoming my usual transport, a dark van. Heavily tinted windows at the front and no windows at the back, it's impossible to see into the van, which lends it a distinctly sinister look.

Allison opens the back of the van for Caitlin and me. I'm first to jump in the back. Caitlin is barely through the door before Allison slams the sliding door shut and jumps into the front seat. She leans back and passes a black military style sub machine gun to me from a well-worn duffle bag.

"What the fuck am I supposed to do with this?" I ask, more frightened by it than anything else.

Erik leans back and points towards the barrel. "You point this end at the bad guys and look serious. Let's hope that's all it takes."

Fantastic, I can't see this going wrong at all. The gun steel is icy cold and a lot heavier than expected. A metaphor for the mess I've gotten myself into. I hold it nervously as Erik pulls the van out of the parking lot.

With no side windows, it's difficult to get an idea of how long we drive towards this place. Then again, I didn't think to ask exactly where this place was. This is far too unplanned for my liking. But the thought of losing Cara is terrifying. I won't lose her; not to those soldiers, not to anyone.

Caitlin looks so unemotional sitting across from me. Yet, under the mask, she struggles to hide her fears. In a way, it makes her seem more fragile. Like the mask will shatter at any moment and she'll fall apart. I hope she holds.

"So ok, point the guns at the bad guys, save the day, it's a great plan and all; but seriously, there are only four of us and I'm not exactly the soldier type," Caitlin says.

"And neither am I," I kick in.

"Do you even know where we need to go?" she asks.

"I saw the maps before," Erik says with a nod. "Allison and I have that covered. Don't worry. All we need you to do is keep watch outside while we deal with what's inside. We'll have the element of surprise, and if we keep a bit of speed to what we're doing we'll have no issues. If it's necessary, there are additional people we can call in if we feel like we more firepower. But from experience these kidnappings tend to be by small teams and the best tactic is to hit them hard and fast before they're able to react or get reinforcements."

"I guess that makes sense." I say.

"Well, we're almost there, so get ready. This is going to happen quickly. Wait for Allison and me to go in. Stand outside until we give the ok to come in," he says.

The van swerves violently as Erik rips the wheel to the left. Allison reaches over and taps on the seat in front of us.

"Heads up."

She's already half out her door as the van screeches to a halt.

Caitlin tears the van's sliding door open, using far too much force. She's running off before it clicks in my mind that I too need to be running with them.

"Shit." I jump out of the van trying not to look stupid.

Thankfully they haven't gone too far ahead. Caitlin points towards the motel door nearest to us. Erik and Allison take up position on either side of the door while Erik points at the number to silently double check with Caitlin that it's the right one. Caitlin nods to them impatiently.

Erik places his hand over the door handle and, with a thump of telekinetic force, flings the door open. Wood around the lock explodes into splinters. Allison is into the room milliseconds behind the door opening.

One hand locks the small machine gun to her shoulder while the other is held out, palm forward, ready to perform any telekinesis. Erik is quickly into the room behind her. I have my arm around Caitlin to try and stop her from running in. So much for keeping watch.

"Shit." The first noise to come from the room is Erik swearing.

Allison shouts out that it's clear. Caitlin breaks free from my grip and runs into the room without a second thought. With nothing else to do I find myself tentatively stepping into the room to see what's going on.

In the middle of the room, Cara lies on a bed face down with a black bag over her head. She struggles against ropes that tie her wrist and ankles together. Caitlin tries to calm her down and get the bag off her head while Erik attempts to use a small pocketknife to cut her free of the ropes without cutting her while she struggles.

A gentle hand on Cara's shoulder seems to help her quiet a little. Erik is first to take advantage, sawing through the heavy ropes to free her hands. He moves down to free her ankles as Caitlin finally gets the bag off her head. Cara mumbles incoherently into the duct tape across her mouth. Despite the recognition in her eyes, they're still wide open in panic. Caitlin tries to gently tear the tape from her lips. It stills leaves a red mark across her face.

Between heavy breaths, with eyes still wide open she cries out, "Run, you need to run."

With One Stone

"Why did you come for me?" She says, devastated. She sluggishly gets to her feet, unsteady as she moves away from the bed.

"What's wrong, Cara?" I ask. Why would she be so upset with our presence?

"They drugged me and left me as bait, you fools. Why else would they leave me here all alone? Please, you've got to get out of here. I don't want you to get hurt because of me."

To punctuate her point, the sound of multiple vehicles fills the room as they pull up outside. Too late. Boots hit concrete as Allison and Erik rush from the room with guns raised. They stand resolutely outside the room, statues against an inevitable flood. Then I watch their resolve fail them. They lower their guns, letting them fall to the ground and dropping their heads in turn, defeated. They couldn't have done otherwise.

With an arm under Cara, I hold her steady as we walk out together. Twenty men, guns raised, stand arrayed against us. There's little chance of avoiding our fate now.

"Well, well. Four little birdies caught with one stone." Levia taunts.

I barely feel Cara recoil in pain as I squeeze her hand I'm holding tightly. I almost pull her off her feet as I tense in anger when Levia takes another step towards us.

"This is a good day. A number of significant members of the resistance all caught together. I think we might even make a special exception for you lot, because as tempted as I am to execute you all on the spot this could be quite the propaganda scoop. It'll let us put a face to the terrorists. Show the public the consequences of complacency.

"Well don't just stand there! Take them all into custody before they decide to do something stupid. Cuff them all," she says, before pointing towards me, "but make sure you put that one out."

Two soldiers step forward. One grabs me by the arm and roughly pulls me from Cara. I watch as the other swings the butt of his gun into her stomach. The last I see of her is the soldier grabbing her by the hair as she doubles over. The pain on her face tells a different story to just having her hair pulled. Then I'm pushed to the ground, face scraping against the concrete.

Allison puts up a brief struggle. She elbows one in the head when his hands wander too far. That earns her a punch in the face and a short trip to the pavement beside me.

I can almost feel each grain of dirt on the pavement grinding against my cheek. I definitely feel the prick of the needle as it enters my neck. Then the world is black once more.

Torture Makes the Heart Grow Fonder

The shock of waking up sends a jolt of adrenaline through me. The room is pitch-black.

Despite the darkness, I can tell I'm in an all-too-familiar setting. Barred window, solid steel door and a soreness in my muscles remind me that the past few days haven't been just a dream.

Memories of the last time spent in a cell like this come flooding back; even a few I must have shut out. A shudder passes through me as I remember the abuse. It is cold comfort to know those guards can't hurt me again.

The room freezes over, as unwelcoming as the last cell. Claustrophobia sets in. Naked; copper bracelets dig painfully into my back. My wrists are on fire, hands numb, locked behind me by thick plastic cuffs.

I try to calm my breathing. For a moment I wonder whether I just haven't left the same nightmare.

No, this isn't the same room. There's something different; somebody else in the room. I hear the sound of their breathing across the room. I listen nervously. The darkness makes me hyper-aware. A moment later and I realise that it's the sound of somebody softly breathing in their sleep. Who are they? Is it safe to try and wake them up? I sit myself up. Feet over the edge of the bed. I manage to stand up, with some difficulty.

Then the door handle rattles. Again? Maybe that's what woke me? My heartbeat races, I remember what happens next. Where's the bed gone? The lights flick on just as the door opens. Instant blindness. Light drilling into the back of my eyes, pain I could do without right now.

Slowly my vision returns. A dark shape hovers in front of me. My eyes focus, just in time to see that the dark shape is the butt of a rifle. It smashes into my nose, sending me flying backwards. I hit the concrete hard.

I find myself lying face first on the concrete floor, my eyes struggling to focus on the blood dripping from my nose. My head spins.

"Get up, please get up. You need to get up," Cara's voice begs me, twisted and distorted.

A thought in the back of my mind tells me to listen. Try, at least for her. It's a battle with the agony spreading beyond my nose. Not fast enough; a boot connects with my ribs, sending me hurtling against the bed.

I lay there, dazed; eyes open, without any recognition of what surrounds me. It's a quick surrender to the pain. With a certain numb curiosity I watch the trail of blood that follows me as they drag me by my ankles out of the room.

Just as I start to find some semblance of coherency somebody props me up into a sitting position. Tape applied roughly to my lips reignites the pain in my face. A black cotton bag gets shoved roughly over my head; a painful return to the black void. The metallic taste of blood overwhelms the only sense I have left.

Cara whimpers as she's dragged next to me. And it kills me that I'm powerless to do anything for her. She's there, only inches beside me and if only I could reach out and touch her, let her know I'm here and she'll be ok. But she may as well be half the world away. At least I won't have to lie.

Boot steps echo, moving off down the hallway. I lose track of time, of how long we're left here. There is a silence that hangs over us, punctuated sporadically by Cara's soft sobbing. The silence tortures; I'm helpless. Time, dispassionate, drags on.

The boots return. I struggle to draw breath through the grip my heart has around my throat. Somebody lifts me into a standing position. With a rough shove they face me in an unknown direction.

"Walk," the captor says bluntly.

I blindly shuffle forward. It sounds like there are more of us here than just Cara and me.

'They need to be cleaned up," Levia says. "Take the females to the showers at the end of the hall. Take the male to the other wing. There are gowns for them to wear until we can get them processed."

A hard shove sends me stumbling forward. I manage only a few ungraceful steps before falling face first to the floor. I'm left prone on the ground for a moment. To humiliate me I suppose. Behind me somebody is laughing. Eventually somebody pulls me back to my feet and shoves me onto a hard plastic seat.

"One at a time! That one first!" a new female voice commands.

A chair scraps across the room. A muffled protest. Not me. I guess that means I wait.

A high pressure shower is turned on in another room. A door shuts and the sound is muffled out.

The darkness that envelopes me is fascinating. It's strange how impossible it is to describe the colours one sees when there is only darkness. Hypnotic. It feels like each colour flashing by represents the last fleeting glimpse into the reality draped around me. As each colour slips from my mind I feel myself slip further into the abyss of darkness. It's my only escape.

♦

Somebody pulls off the cloth bag covering my head. Light floods back into my world; a not-so-subtle reminder that reality won't stand for escapees. I'm surrounded by guards with guns pointed at me. Directly in front of me is a door to the next room.

The shower is switched off. Allison is dragged out of the door, a guard tightly holding each of her arms. She flashes me a look of defiance. All I'm able to do is look directly back at her and meet her eyes. And I so desperately want to smile at her and tell her I understand. I hope she can tell through this tape.

My eyes wander over her. The gown put on her hides nothing. She has the kind of body that makes me

130

instantly jealous; athletic and strong. My face flushes, hot. Yet she also carries a set of scars that hold a story that's begging to be told. I find myself staring at her, unabashed. She's sat in the chair next to me, completely composed. She gives me a subtle nod, a tilt of her chin to show she isn't broken. Her defiant beauty lifts me. If she remains strong then perhaps all is not lost.

Then it's my turn. A guard steps forward and lifts me out of the chair. Another joins him and together they drag me into the other room.

A woman stands in front of me and with a hand on each cheek starts pressing around my nose, poking and prodding without any semblance of gentleness. The pain makes my eyes water.

"Lucky you, it's not broken," She says indifferently.

If she presses any damn harder, I suspect it will break just to make her stop, out of sympathy for me. She picks at the corner of the tape over my mouth. Then to cement how little sensitivity she has for me, tears it off with one quick pull. I flinch in pain. She just gives an unsympathetic grunt and pushes me into an area of tiled floor.

"Sit down," she orders me.

The guards waiting behind her raise their guns to ensure I know I have no say in the matter. The floor is wet and freezing cold. Then water hits me. I try to crawl away from the frigid water that batters me. But with my arms locked behind my back there's no avoiding it. In seconds I'm shivering. Somebody squirts some sort of liquid soap haphazardly over me. All I can do is curl up as they painfully scrub me. They drag the brushes over my face, leaving me coughing and spluttering; the water bitter.

At some point the brushes stop and I'm left on the freezing tiles. I try hard to keep thinking of Allison's defiance; to stay composed in the face of apparent helplessness. I fail, miserably. I feel each icy drop of water hit me. Each steals a little more of the warmth that Cara, Allison and everyone else had shown me in the past few days.

I'm lost in the forest near our house. Mum and Dad were distracted. They wouldn't pay attention to me.

A memory from before my parent's death; a memory of a day I had long forgotten. That day something important happened, though the significance I can't seem to recall. I remember the jealousy, the rage; at least as much jealousy and rage as my little five-year-old self could muster. It seems so petty to me now, but back then it meant so much. I ran away. It never occurred to me, so young, what I was going to do after I ran away. I just ran. We'd never been allowed to play in this forest. It was too dangerous, Dad said. Too easy to get lost. So my little five-year-old self found out.

Under the cover of the trees it starts to get dark quickly. The sun struggles to filter through the heavy foliage. The trees begin close in around me like the claws of the demons from my nightmares. Behind every tree lies a hungry animal waiting to eat me. Every noise becomes the growl of an evil beast waiting to kill me. I curl up under a tree and start crying.

Somewhere under all the water pouring over me, all that's left the lost little girl, crying. How much more will they throw at me? How much more before I'm lost forever?

The water shuts off. I'm completely numb. I can't feel anything beyond tears. I don't understand how Allison can be so defiant. This seems hopeless to me.

They drag me away from the shower and leave me lying in the middle of the cold tile floor whilst they rub towels roughly over me. I'm not sure if it's a poor attempt to dry me, or just further abuse they want me to endure. The rough towels make poor work of it. Eventually it stops and I'm lifted to my feet again.

A guard slices off the cuffs around my wrists. I can feel their hesitation as they do it; were it not for the fact that it would be impossible to get this thin hospital gown on me I'm sure they would have left me cuffed. It sticks to my still damp skin, which compounds the difficulty getting it on. In the end they just pull on it harder, roughly tying it off once they finally get it on.

My arms are quickly twisted behind me so that they can click the cuffs back on. I'm not sure what their concern is. I couldn't fight back even if I really did feel like getting myself killed.

Levia tapes my mouth up again. She then slaps me, hard, across the face. I'm so numb I don't even feel it. That seems to upset her.

"Bah, take her back into the other room, bag her and bring one of the twins in." She says angrily.

A guard gives me a hard shove from behind, sending me scrambling through the door. Without the bag over

133

my head I'm finally able to get a look at Cara, to see if she's ok. She sits slumped in the dark blue plastic chair with another of the black cotton bags over her head.

Of her porcelain-white skin, it makes an austere counter to the deep colour of her seat; her pale and faultless complexion enhanced only by her deep rose nipples centred bold on the rest of her petit breasts. My eyes roam lower, finding the only other blemish to her pale skin. It occurs to me how easily I'm abusing her dignity.

Her sister sits beside her with a lot more confidence; legs spread and feet firmly anchored on the ground. Sharing Cara's unblemished skin, Caitlin differs only by virtue of a pair of colourful tattoos adorning each shoulder and in the fact that her current posture leaves little to the imagination.

Another guard takes the bag off covering Cara's head. Her face is red and slick with tears; her left cheek bruising. My curiosity towards her nakedness turns quickly to horror at my own thoughts as I think about what Cara went through only moments ago. I silently castigate myself for the hypocrisy of my focus. It's in that moment that I get what Allison was trying to instil in me. Cara needs to know that all is not lost. Trying my best to hide my own fears, I look her in the eyes. I can see her searching me for answers as she looks straight back at me. This tape makes it impossible to see me smile, but maybe it's enough. Not that I'm able to read her face to see if I'm convincing. I hold her eyes as I take my seat without fuss. I don't want to give them a chance to force a show of weakness while she's watching. For the next few minutes, she's going to need all the strength she can get. Then my world turns dark again as the black bag is replaced over my head.

It's an anxious wait as I hear them walk her into the other room and shut the door, the sound of the shower muted as the door clicks shut.

Time crawls, until the shower eventually stops and Cara is dragged back into the room. Does she see me? I hear her drop heavily into her seat. What does that mean? Is she ok? Not being able to see her is driving me crazy.

"Hurry up! This is taking too long." Levia says.

A chair scatters across the room followed by a struggle of desperate feet scraping the floor. Don't struggle Caitlin. A loud thud cuts the struggling short. All that follows is another uneasy wait.

Mum picks up Claire again. I look out from my hiding spot under the bed. I was being quiet just like Mum wants. I watch her desperately try to convince Claire to hide, but she didn't seem to understand why she couldn't help. Maybe she thought it was just a game. I didn't understand what was going on either at the time. I just knew that I had to follow what Mum said and be quiet.

I could be quiet for her.

She tells Claire to hide under the bed. She begs her. Her voice sounds so much more desperate, remembering it now.

"No mummy, I have to protect them," Claire says, shaking her head.

There's a loud bang as the bedroom door explodes inward.

Two hands pull me out of my memory, gripping me too firmly under each arm to lift me to my feet. A voice tells me succinctly to walk. More pushing and shoving gets me heading in the direction they want.

"Take them to the main entrance for processing. Keep the hoods on them until you get there. Given all the trouble this one caused last time she was here, they'll be going to the high security area so that they can be better guarded and away from the other residents here."

One Problem at a Time

"Always with the hoods, always with those damn hoods," a new voice says. "Let me guess, they're taped up too?"

"You know it's the security protocol when moving captives about," the woman says.

"And beating them is also part of that protocol?"

Nothing is said in response. The hood is pulled off. I'm standing in a hall filled with tables and benches. The man who spoke stands in front of us; older than us but not by much, a sharp face with black hair slicked back. He wears his uniform without the air of formality the guards behind him have.

"Here, let me get that off you," the man says as he tries to gently peel the tape off my mouth. There's no gentle way to do it, but it's a relief at least. He un-cuffs me, then repeats the process with the others.

He steps back to address us. "Right, I'm the warden of this facility. As you well know, you're here at the mercy of the Templars. As you by now can tell, they are not interested in playing nice. Some are still chaffing from the last time you were a guest of the Templars and are eager for retribution. At all times follow the directions the guards give you. Needless to say, if you try anything or if you attempt to escape they'll shoot you.

"You'll each be assigned a room off the main courtyard and be allocated separate times for use of the exercise yard. Otherwise, you'll be in solitary rooms. Take in your friend's faces, because it'll be the last time you see them for a while. Please don't find out the consequences of attempting otherwise. Know that you will be monitored.

"Anyone found without their bracelets or any other device that they are required to wear will be assumed dangerous and summarily shot. No questions asked. If you cooperate with us I will do what I can to make your stay here short and reasonably comfortable. Avoid making it unnecessarily shorter by attracting the guard's attention.

"Now, if you'll all follow me to your cells, in them you'll find clothing you will need to wear."

He opens the doors of the hall and leads us out to a rectangular courtyard. Surrounding the courtyard is the concrete facility with what appear to be cells on every side. A covered walkway wraps around the outside of the courtyard, but the yard itself is open to the air, a large grassy park complete with trees and even a bird fountain. It's such beautiful sanctuary, so incompatible with the bleak surrounds.

We stop in front of the first room. He twists the handle on the half a foot steel door. It slides open.

"This is you," he says pointing to me. "It's all automatic. Twist the handle and it has an assisted opening that does the work for you. And when you close it, you just need to get it started and it'll slide itself closed. It's locked and unlocked during the day on a timer. You'll hear a five minute warning alarm each shift change. If you're caught outside when the doors lock and a guard has to let you in, there will be consequences.

"Next to the main hall is the library if you're looking for something to do. You can take books from there to your room."

He turns from me. "Now let's get the rest of you to your rooms."

The door slides shut behind me once I step into the room, cutting me off from the world.

The room is just a long narrow corridor. Against the left wall is a bed, beside which is barely enough space to pass.

Beyond the bed is a desk with a couple of books piled on it and a plastic chair tucked underneath. After another metre or so of empty space, the far left corner of the room is sectioned off behind a small wall. The wall itself is covered in polished stainless steel, acting as a poor mirror. It's a little too claustrophobic for my liking. I've slept in worse places though.

"What the hell have I gotten myself into?" I say out loud. The walls don't answer.

A stack of clothes is arranged neatly on the bed; a familiar looking pair of utilitarian navy pants and matching long-sleeved button-up shirt. At least they're better than this useless gown. I strip off and stand naked in front of the steel mirror. I close my eyes as my hands slide down my body; I imagine it's her for a moment, caressing me gently, touching me. But when I open my eyes the girl in the mirror is fuzzy and distorted. Tired and battered. A sigh as I put on the briefs that lay tucked at the bottom of the clothing pile. I suppose it doesn't matter now. Next is a poor excuse for a bra. Or maybe it's just a short tank top? I can't tell. It's not like I have anything in the way of curves to fill it anyway. Why would she settle for something this broken? At least the pants fit.

A buzzer goes off as I finish buttoning the navy shirt. The cell door slides open with a loud click. This must be my little piece of scheduled freedom. Grabbing a book from the small pile on the cell desk, I put on the slip-on shoes that wait next to the bed and tentatively step out of the cell. It turns out that freedom for somebody as tired as me isn't much different than confinement, there's just more sun involved. Still, I find a comfortable spot under a tree to start reading. The bark of the tree I'm leaning against is worn smooth, the grass underneath surprisingly soft; this comfortable spot is, I'm guessing, a popular place for others to spend their time. This would be a nice place to relax were it not for the cold surroundings of this concrete jail.

The book struggles to hold my attention. The lead heroine is well developed, but the plot, right from the start, is contrived. As I read further, I develop the feeling that the lead character deserves a better story than the one this author has given her. I mostly skim through the book, bored, but with nothing else I can do. The sun is a warm blanket wrapped around me.

"Hello there," a young voice says from around the other side of the tree. A girl, mid-teens, pokes her head around the tree, dark hair hanging over the curious smile on her face. "Why are you sitting here, all alone?"

What choice do I have?

"You have choices. You're just holding onto the restraints," she reaches up and taps me on the side of the head, "up here so tightly, you can't see them. You can't get them off because you believe you can't get them off. Stop listening what your mind tells you the rules are. You hold back because you're afraid of failing. This façade you've constructed to protect you from everything you've had to go through, it's holding you back and it's time to tear it down. Expose yourself to the unknown, the abyss. Stare it down. Stop blaming yourself for everything that has happened, find Claire and get out of this place."

"And how do I do that with these on?" I say, waving my braceletted wrists at her, frustrated. "And even if I do get them off, then what? I barely know how to control my talent."

"The rumours say otherwise."

"I had help, I wasn't in control."

"Had help? How could you have had help? They're attuned to the wearer. It has to be the wearer that gets them off. It's the wearer that must let go of their restraints. Nobody else can do that for them."

"I definitely had help." I insist.

She just shrugs. "Then I don't know," she says. "Think about it. I need to go; I've already spent too long here. Before I leave you to your sleep, your friend Cara; your talents aren't the only thing you need to stop holding back."

She moves as if to step back around the tree.

"Wait, before you leave, how do you know who I am?"

"One problem at a time."

She slips behind the tree before I can ask her name. I follow her around the tree but she's nowhere to be seen.

I see Mum in the distance, standing at the edge of the trees, holding a wrapped up bundle in her arms. Dad is beside her, he has Claire in his arms. It's only been a few minutes but it feels like a lifetime to my four year old self. I hear Mum and Dad calling out for me. Claire is pointing in my direction and jumping excitedly in Dad's arms. I run towards them as quickly as my little legs can take me. Dad smiles at me and pats me gently on the head when I reach them.

Even then, at five-years-old, Claire knew exactly where to find me.

"We're really lucky Claire knew where to find you." He says without a hint of the anger I was expecting. *'She and you are going to be inseparable. Now why did you run away like that?"*

"I thought you were going to send me away and that my replacement had just arrived."

"Aww, don't be silly." Mum says. "We're not replacing you. And we'd never send you away."

Mum's expression suddenly turns serious. She and Dad share a look of worry. Then they start to rush us back towards home. "Come on everyone, quickly quickly, we need to get back to the house right away."

Self Discovery

A buzzer fills the courtyard, pulling me, unwillingly, from my sleep. My back is killing me and I feel absolutely exhausted; this tree was a lot more comfortable when I first sat down. The courtyard is still empty, but for a pair of guards in the distance. I watch as one of them walks over to me. He's older than me, certainly, but with his sandy brown hair and a soft face that lacks the hard edge the other soldiers have, he comes across as young, barely an adult. But in a place like this? It's an illusion, a deception.

"That buzzer is the warning to tell you that you need to return to your cell. If the other guards see you out here, well..." he shakes his head. "Just head back quickly now. I'll bring your meal to you shortly."

He holds his arm out in a gesture to help me up. I help myself up. He shrugs.

The sound of the lock on the massive door to my cell echoes throughout the room as it clicks shut. The place feels empty. More than just physically. I sit, exhausted on the bed, my mind unfocused.

Moments later, the cell door slides open again.

144

"Here, I brought your dinner," he says. "I have to be honest though, the food here is pretty terrible. I snuck in a chocolate drink for you, to try to make it bearable."

He carefully places the tray of food on the bed beside me and returns to the doorway.

Do you have a name?" he asks, hopeful.

I sit silently, head ducked, trying to avoid conversation. What does he want from me? I just want to finish reading my book. No, that's a lie. Right now all I can think about is Cara.

"That bad, huh?" he says. He sighs, dejectedly. "Try not let being inside this place get to you. We're not all bad, I promise."

Really? You could have fooled me. I stare at him, annoyed. And I want to scream at him, yell at him with all my anger. But tired as I am, I don't want to make things worse.

"Ok, I get the hint. I'll be back in the morning with your breakfast."

He turns and heads out of the cell, his warm smile tinged surprisingly with a trailing hint of remorse. On the tray, some nondescript meat and other colourless portions compete to see which pile of sludge is the most disgusting. Still, it's better than what I've seen some street vendors offload in the stalls of the abandoned suburbs. Nevertheless, I spend more time playing with the food than eating it. It's just so... boring. If I wasn't so damn hungry I wouldn't bother at all. Most of the food I can't identify. It all tastes the same.

When I'm finished I throw the tray at the door in frustration. A mini act of rebellion, for what it's worth.

145

With nothing better to do, I try returning to reading. Unsuccessfully. I keep slipping into a daydream as I play out different scenarios of escape with Cara. Pure fantasy. I shouldn't hold false hopes. Before long, I throw the book into the corner in bored frustration and try curling up to sleep.

♦

Soldiers rush through the door, guns raised.

"Don't move!" The first one yells as he runs in.

Mum stands protectively in front of Claire. A black shadow lashes out from her and pierces through the man's throat. He takes one more step before falling forward. He lies awkwardly, his dead eyes open staring directly at me.

A gun behind him goes off. Shadows strike out from mother as she wraps herself protectively around Claire. Another man falls through the door, dead. The shadows dance around her, trying to protect her. More guns fire.

Dad rushes in from the other room. He calls to her. No Dad, run away. More guns fire. More men die.

Everything goes quiet. Mum lies curled around Claire; the shadows now silent. Dad stumbles, falls to his knees. A boot kicks Dad out of the way. Hands drag Mum's lifeless body away from my sister. I want to scream. A soldier bends down to pick Claire up. From my hiding spot I watch him lift her up to take her away. I want to run out and attack him. Claire looks at me, calm, and shakes her head.

146

"...no." I whisper.

I take a deep breath and open my eyes. It must have been a nightmare, another memory from my childhood. The room is dark. I have to get out of here. I have to find my sister. All I've managed to do so far is get more people hurt, captured. Just like I got my parents hurt. Just like I got my own sister captured. If only I hadn't have run off that day. Instead of having to spend the time finding me, they would have been better prepared for the attack. We all might have escaped together. And how did I repay my sister for finding me that day? I got her locked up with these psychopaths. I can't imagine how frightened she must have been.

Staring at the ceiling it's clear I'll not get back to sleep again. Was I just fooling myself thinking I could free my sister? Am I just fooling myself thinking Cara will ever want me?

A female voice fills the room. "A fool, perhaps, but not for those reasons," she says. "Not as foolish as your sister thinking she could keep you safe from here forever."

A black figure materialises in the dark room, sitting on the desk with her legs swinging playfully over the edge.

"But we are all fools in one way or another," she says. "I'm sorry I didn't get the chance to introduce myself the last time we met. I'm Macha. Now, where's my sister Nemain? What's her excuse this time?"

"You mean Nem? I haven't seen her since yesterday."

"If she gives me some bull about those bracelets I'll slap her upside the head. This is typical of her, always leaving me to do her work for her."

"Speak for yourself," Nem pipes up angrily, appearing in the corner of the room.

"Shit, how long have you been there?" I exclaim.

"Girl, don't you get it? Unless you send me away, I'm always with you."

"You were there the whole time?" I say.

"Of course."

"Why didn't you help us when we were captured? They could have killed us!" I scream at her.

"I would have stepped in if necessary. I thought it was... character building," Nem says. "You could easily have gotten out of that situation. Anyway, you're inside their Keep now, isn't that what you wanted?"

"They had guns and there were lots more of them than us! And if you can't tell, I'm not exactly free to wander around this place!"

"So? I can't do everything for you."

"I take it that includes getting these things off?" I ask.

"Is your one this slow?" Nem asks Macha.

Macha laughs. "Oh yes, they're definitely cut from the same cloth."

Nem turns back to me. "Look, I am you, a manifestation of your power. I'm totally at the mercy of your power. And while you believe those bracelets hold sway over you, while you choose to limit your energy and your control over it, there's nothing much I can do for you. On this side of the veil, you are as much my gateway as I am yours to the other.

"I think this is a good lesson, in some ways; learning to use your abilities blindly. You can't always trust what your mind is telling you. And your talent is just another sense. There are people out there capable of manipulating your very perception of the world. You have to trust in your abilities and trust what your intuition tells you. You have so much potential waiting for you to find. You just have to stop holding back. Stop being afraid. This wall you're hiding behind to protect yourself. Break it down."

"I've heard those words already today." I say, curious. "Were you the little girl in the courtyard earlier today?"

"What girl in the courtyard? You walked outside, sat down under that tree and promptly fell asleep," Nem says.

"I swear, while I was out there, there was a girl who came up to me and spoke to me."

"It wasn't my or mine's doing," Macha says.

"Curious. Perhaps it was your subconscious predicting the future," Nem says.

"Maybe," Macha says. "Did the girl in your dream look like you?"

"She was a few years younger than me, but yes, she did look vaguely familiar. She had red hair just like mine. She could have been me five years ago. Why didn't I recognise that at the time? That's really weird."

"Curiouser and Curiouser, don't you think?" Nem says to Macha.

"One problem a time," Macha responds cryptically.

"That's what she said!"

"Look, just forget about that for the moment. Let's concentrate on getting you out of here. Why don't we try something?" Nem says. Then, taking one of the books from the desk, throws it at my head. I prevent it from hitting the wall behind me by stopping it with my forehead.

"Shit!" I yell. "Ow!"

"She really is slow," Macha laughs.

"How about giving me time to prepare next time?" I ask.

"Time to prepare!" they exclaim, simultaneously.

"You don't get 'time to prepare' in the real world," Macha says.

Nem throws another book at me. This time I see it coming and manage to duck out of the way.

"While I get your point, it's who the fuck knows what in the morning, can't it wait?" I ask angrily.

"No, it really can't fucking wait. But I can see you're tired and that's going to make things difficult. Shall we leave the sleepy one to her beauty sleep?" Nem asks, tossing another book to herself.

"Hmm, not sure it's a good idea to wait. You have to understand that in this war, you may not get the chance tomorrow," Macha says.

"Look where I am. My war was over not long after it started," I argue.

"Girl, your war has only just begun," Nem says, flipping the book again. "But the truth is, sometimes it's sleep that you end up missing the most in times like this."

"Don't do anything stupid," Macha says before disappearing.

"Or at least, try not to get yourself killed while doing something stupid," Nem says. Then she launches another book at me before vanishing herself.

The room darkens. Whether stupidity or shock, I watch the book intently as it travels at an impossibly slow speed towards me. The way it tumbles through the air towards me is curious. In a lot of ways it's just like me, tumbling out of control towards inevitable disaster. The thought draws a smile. Of course, the inevitable disaster in this case is going to be it smashing into my nose, an unpleasant experience I'd rather avoid repeating. If only we could just let go of our inevitable fate and just step into something completely different. But by the time we realise we need to, life smacks us on the nose for being too slow and it's too late to change. If only we could freeze time, for just a second, to take a moment to think.

The book stops an inch in front of my nose. For just that moment, time belongs to me. And for just that moment I know I have my second.

Then the second runs out. The book smacks me hard on the nose; a polite reminder that when we get our second to change destiny, we shouldn't sit there staring idly at it.

I lie down to try sleeping again; uncertain the throbbing pain in my face was a fair price for the lesson learnt.

The door to my cell slides open. Light floods in through the doorway. The soldier from yesterday stands in the doorway.

"Can I come in?" he asks, waiting patiently.

"Sure," I say, giving up avoiding speaking with him.

He steps inside the doorway, but enters no further.

"Wow, your face looks terrible... err, I mean, you're pretty bruised up. Um, shit, well... I brought you your breakfast and lunch for later, as well as a change of clothes. I also brought you this book I thought you might enjoy."

He waits for a response, uncertain. Finally, maybe realising he won't get one, he says, "Well, I'll just put them on your bed then and leave you too it."

He turns his back to me and walks out. The moment the door slides shut I jump at the food, starving. It's warm and palatable. Better than expected, actually enjoyable.

On the other hand, the shower is unbearable. Every position of the taps give the same temperature – Icy cold. I spend as little time as necessary under it. By the end I'm shivering and stiff. Not an experience I will get used to.

I quickly get dressed and wrap myself up in my bed's sole woollen blanket, to warm up. The blanket is rough and scratchy, but at least it's warm.

Picking up the book he left, I prop up the pillow against the wall and lean back. Something to distract myself from the tedium. The book, *Friday*, is ancient;

its spine long since broken, pages deep brown with age. And made from real, actual paper. Not the plastic substitute they use these days. I quickly get lost in the story.

It works for a while; in spite of my thoughts the book is enjoyable and I read a few chapters in. But, despite my attempts to stay focused, my thoughts wander; getting further and further distracted with thoughts of Cara. Right now I can't seem to focus on the story. Another time, perhaps?

The words of the girl in the courtyard weigh on me. Does Cara really feel that way about me? Maybe the girl is right. I want to hold Cara so badly. Stand behind her and wrap my arms around her. Kiss her. Slide my hands down her body. I've never felt this way about anyone before.

I shift myself in bed a little; heart beating a little quicker. A bottom lip bitten in pleasure. What's gotten into me?

What does it matter, I want this. I want her. Breathe. Exhale. I close my eyes and curl up.

Time Abandons Me

The door to my cell slides open. I don't know how long I slept. A silhouette in the doorway blocks the fading light. I bolt upright, instantly awake.

"Oh, don't panic now, little girl," the familiar voice of Levia says. She steps inside so I can see her. "I've just come for a little chat. Here, I brought you breakfast." She places a tray of food on the table and sits down on the bed.

"Come, sit here." She pats the bed beside here. Her tone is polite, but her eyes suggest I have little choice.

"If you give me what I want, I'm sure I could do a lot for you," she says, leaning closer.

She wraps her arm around me and strokes my arm. This is awkward. What could she possible want?

"I can make your time here a lot more comfortable. More free time, hot food all the time." She whispers into my ear, "I'll even promise to release your friends, if you do what I ask."

Then she slides her hand between my legs, groping me forcefully. "Do you get my drift?"

"What the fuck?" I yell at her, shoving her away from me, hard.

Her wicked laugh rolls through the room. She rushes towards me, grabbing me by the throat and shoving me against the wall. She crushes my neck into the wall, fire sweeps through my lungs, burning for air.

"You'll help me, one way or the other."

The world dims as I feel myself starting to pass out. The two black forms of Nem and Macha appear behind her. They step towards her, eyes glowing brightly.

"Too easy," Levia whispers into my ear.

Nem and Macha make it no closer. Levia throws me to the ground. In my blurry vision I see them twitching, flickering unstably between crow and human forms. Wicked laughter joins with Levia's.

"A fine catch," Levia says, fiendishly.

"Guards! Get in here! Take her and the others down to the basement level. It's time this little one learns the consequences of her choices."

A guard pulls his pistol out and pushes the barrel forcefully to my temple.

"If you move, if you struggle, if you cry out, I'll kill you."

The world goes black as a heavy sack is shoved over my head. With my arms pinned behind my back, they lift me out of my cell. Why can't they just let me walk? It's raining in the courtyard, a heavy, steady rain. Cold drops splash on me as they drag me away. I used to enjoy listening to the rain, once.

Then I'm inside again. Thankfully they let me walk myself down the stairs though it's a difficult prospect with this damn bag over my head.

A few stumbles later I'm at the bottom of stairs. After what seems like a long maze of turns impossible to keep up with, a guard grabs my shoulder, stopping me. I feel him tense, misunderstanding his intention, until a blow hits me behind knee, crumpling me to the floor. I'm lifted back to my feet and left standing, confused and uncertain, for a torturous few minutes; the noise of activity around me muffled heavily by the bag over my head. The pain subsides, eventually.

The sack is finally pulled off my head. It was starting to get unbearable. Sweat drips down my neck. I stand alone, but for the soldiers guarding me. The room is large and unfamiliar; lit by hundreds of candles that fill iron chandeliers hanging over a plush blood-red carpet running through the centre of the worn-smooth stone floor. Red crosses on white banners decorate each wall. The aisle leads to a platform that rises in steps in front of me. Arranged around a simple wooden podium centred on the platform are three overly ornate thrones, each covered with gold icons and emblems while further red-crossed white banners drape each arm. The decorations adorning the room and the gaudy thrones stand out, in excess, against the temple's soft stone.

Cold steel is pressed against my throat. "Don't fucking move. Keep your mouth shut. Don't say a word unless somebody asks you a question. No second chances," a guard spits.

Three old men shuffle in from the darkness beyond the platform, their ash grey uniforms as ornate and pretentious as the thrones. The white band around each arm reflects their loyalties. They seat themselves but avoid looking at me, scanning the room but refusing to look in my direction.

One by one, soldiers bring the others in, through the halls massive steel doors, and stand them next to me. Erik is first, standing resolutely behind me, pain clear through gritted teeth. Allison, stood beside him, pushes her luck as they take the bag off her head. She takes a swing at her captor as soon as it's off. The guard responds by punching her in the stomach with a sickening thud and she doubles over in pain. Erik reaches down to help her. Steel flashes in the candle light, pressed threateningly against their necks to end any further resistance. Cara stands beside me, breathing heavily. Scared. Caitlin leans against Cara. Both stare off into the darkness.

Once we're all inside, many more soldiers file in, filling lines of wooden pews ranked behind us. We stand silent, waiting anxiously for something to happen. The doors open again. A girl screams. "No! Not her. You promised me you would leave her out of this."

It's hard to see what's going on with this lighting. Another group, wearing the same drab uniforms as we do are marched stiffly past us to stand to the side of the platform. They stare blankly at the ground.

There is a commotion at the back of the room, as guards try to restrain someone, kicking and screaming.

Though with all the movement and dim lighting it is impossible to see what's going on.

"You promised me you'd keep her out of this!"

"Enough!" a man shouts, reverberating throughout the hall.

"A suggestion, if I may, Marshal," Levia says as she takes the podium. "If she wishes to join the others so much, why not let her? We have both of them now. She is... no longer required."

The Marshal just waves his hand dismissively. "As you wish."

The girl, beaten, her head hanging dejectedly with hair covering her face is dragged down the aisle of the church. They stand her up beside me. The girl, her familiar face, looks at me, crestfallen.

"My sweet little sister; I tried so hard to keep you out. I didn't want you to get caught up in this. I'm sorry," she whispers.

Her words pierce straight through me. I'm torn three ways – between the joy of finally finding her, fear of the situation we're in and my own stupidity that all this time, I didn't recognise her. Why not? It was so obvious.

"I'm sorry I didn't find you sooner," I whisper back.

I smile at her, happy to have finally found her, no matter our circumstance. She smiles back; a divine smile to show me that everything will be alright. She doesn't believe it. But today, big sister, today everything will turn out ok. I promise.

"Revered Knights of the Order of the Temple, before you today stand this city's most vile heretics. Five psychics who have hidden themselves away from our government, who have refused to submit to our government and its people. Worse still, they all actively conspire against it.

"Bear witness to their crimes and as this city's exalted representatives pass judgement upon them. Remember today well, as it will be the beginning of a new dawn for this city.

"Not since the end of the war itself has such a large cell of these psychic heretics been caught together. May the responsibility for their judgement rest comfortably on your shoulders."

Levia pulls out a folded piece of paper, her act undoing her military jacket and taking it out exaggerated and dramatic.

"I have here written confessions, signed by the weak minded terrorists before. Not one of them had the strength of conviction to stand by their heresy when faced with the might of the Templars. Weak. Bring them onto the stage!"

Led up the single step onto the platform, we're filed into a line beside the podium. A guard shoves Cara in the back. She stumbles forward. Levia hands her the sheet of paper.

"Speak loudly so everyone can hear you. If you hesitate, your friends behind you will suffer for it."

Cara looks around, scared, panicking, unsure what to do. Allison gives her a stoic nod.

She takes a deep breath, her voice shaking.

"We five..."

"Six now," Levia interrupts. "Continue."

"Freely and willingly admit to the following crimes and place ourselves at the people's mercy for judgement.

"We acknowledge that it was our willing choice to take this path; ignoring the government controls for talented individuals that are designed to protect the community. As a group we used our abilities to conspire and commit to breaking and entering into government facilities and the homes of private individuals. We have used our abilities to steal, purely for our own profits. On multiple occasions we have resisted arrest from lawful individuals. We have shot at and killed people to prevent our capture. On multiple occasions we have wilfully planned the murder of law enforcement and other government officials without any due cause.

"This is just a small fraction of the crimes we have committed over the years. Perhaps, worst of all, we have used our abilities to manipulate the very humanity of those we have come into contact with. All this for our own selfish benefit. We have gotten these benefits at the cost of our souls."

When I think about what Cara is saying, it's all true. That really does sum up what we've done. We are murderers, really. I recoil at the thought.

"I don't think we really need you to finish the rest of that," Levia says. "I think we've heard more than enough of your confession to get the point. Still, I think it's important that everyone here see's the reality of just who you are and just what it is that the government must face. While all they have admitted to are certainly heinous crimes, it is this one in particular which is the most heinous of sins."

"And for that, we are still missing two more guests," a new voice slinks out of the shadows.

Levia flashes Claire and me a wicked smile as the man steps forward. "Meet Lucian. He has been hunting pests. And how has the hunt gone, Lucian?"

He steps forward from the shadows of the platform. A murmur spreads across the room. In each hand he carries a pair sadistically twisted copper cages; two almost dead crows lie twitching at the bottom of the cages. It's only the impossible blackness and the faint glow of red eyes that gives away their supernatural identities. He places them down carefully at the front of the platform for all to see.

"Did you really think your little fairies could outsmart us?"

Levia addresses the crowd. "While all that they have admitted to are certainly heinous crimes, it is this one in particular which is the most heinous of sins." She points aggressively at my sister and me. "These ones, these vile witches, these heretics, who willingly consort with the demons we have captured and locked within these holy cages."

The murmur that had running through the soldiers has now changed to a fever pitch.

"Thank you Seneschal Lucian, Seneschal Levia," the Marshal says. "Without the help you have given to the Templars, without your constant vigilance and tireless dedication to our most holy work, this city and its people might now have been in much worse circumstances."

Levia and Lucian bow reverently to him.

"If we hadn't caught them when we did, soon your very minds and souls would be owned by these wicked fiends." Lucian says, with vigour. "This is why you fought the war more than two decades ago, Marshal. This is the nature of those who are talented and why we must be ever vigilant against them. This is why we must never suffer a heretic to live."

"And so I ask you all," Levia continues, "what judgement is fit for these heretics?"

She takes one step towards Cara. Steel flashes under her jaw. Cara clutches her throat. Crimson blooms through fingertips.

"Only death." She smiles.

Today, time abandons me, running away all too quickly. Cara dies in front of me.

Slip

The floor is cold, hard under my knees. My hands slip on the bloody surface. I'm supposed to feel something, right? So what now? What do I do now? The world is dark. There is nothing left worth seeing. It doesn't register that the people frozen around me isn't natural.

"What if I told you, you could undo what just happened?" Lucian whispers, suddenly standing beside me. The room twists and warps unnaturally around him.

"Within you is the ability to make it happen," he says. "You just need to remember how. Didn't your little birdies tell you that you forgot on purpose? Here, let's start by taking these off."

He touches my wrists. The bracelets unclip and hang in mid-air, frozen in time.

"Can you feel the energy?" he asks.

I can. It washes over me.

"That's just a drop in the ocean of energy available to you. Waiting on the other side of the veil is that ocean and it's all yours if you open the doorway to it. It can offer you so much. I promise you it's easily enough to bring back your friend's life. I can show you how. All you need is open the doorway."

A vision plays out in my head. He shows me how to reverse the damage to Cara; how to reach across the veil, into the past, and pull her life into the present. In the vision I see her breathe again, smiling, happy.

"Why should I believe you?" I ask.

"What choice do you have?" he replies.

"Why show me this?"

"Hmmm, you might say that I enjoy screwing with Levia more than anything else. She shouldn't be the one having all the fun."

And what might the price be, I wonder?

"Price, oh yes, it comes at a price," he says, wickedly. He flickers out of sight. When he reappears he's holding one of the copper cages. A twist and it's open. He pulls out Nem, her crow form twitching in his grip.

"You have a choice," he says, squeezing Nem's body sadistically. "Little Nem here is your gateway to the other side; your link through the veil. A tiny and insignificant gateway. In this world, in this form, she's holding back that power from you. Destroy her. Tear the veil open upon her and it will all flow freely to you, everything she has been holding back from you. Turn on your true potential. All that you've been looking for. Then and only then will you truly be Death as she has claimed you to be. Then and only then will you have the power you seek over it."

"It's your choice. Sacrifice Death herself for the death of your friend. One death for another. Make it quick."

It's an easy choice to make.

"Good." He seems happy with my choice.

The shadows lift. Nem's life lies still in my hands while Cara's life drips from my fingertips. The wall shatters inside my mind. Time finds itself again. Hundreds of black tendrils surround me, all coiling through Nem and seeking the void beyond her. I focus entirely on tearing Nem apart. As twisted it seems, I can see the truth in Lucian's words, the steps to Cara's salvation. The veil shows me the layers of time that wrap around her.

Levia stands over me and Cara. Move. My mind registers the command; a thick tendril of power pushes Levia into the nearest wall. I kneel down to Cara. Hold her. See time wrapped around her. Watch the layers of her timeline peel away from her. Each layer takes a little more effort, a little more power. Each layer pushes my mind further into the veil, tearing at the gateway to that torrent of power, further and further. Claire is screaming at me. It doesn't register; at least at first. I need to focus.

"No sister, no." Her screams fall off to nothing.

But I've already reached the point in Cara's timeline I'm looking for. It comes so quickly, so easily in the end. The point in Cara's timeline I needed to reach. Too easily. A shared breath. Her eyes open. Her recognition. My elation.

It worked; the other side is totally open to me and all its potential is clear. Levia's broken body starts laughing, sinister, and pure evil. Behind me, Lucian takes up the laugher. The room watches intently, everyone frozen.

Where Nem once was, my hands disappear into a large void that envelopes the podium before me. I find myself on my knees staring into a black abyss. And in that moment I see the true price I've paid. The veil and its full potential stands open to me in this world, but now this world is open to the veil. I see hundreds of histories and possibilities laid out in planes before me, stretching to infinity. Beyond my comprehension. And there, stalking energy planes which show neither history nor future are creatures that have no place in this world. Dark and sinister entities. So many... hundreds upon hundreds of them, all waiting, eternally patient, waiting for the wall between our worlds to crumble so they might pour forth into this world, beings possessing intelligence far beyond any human understanding. I see the true nature of Levia and Lucian, and, with horror, the beings that pull the strings of their puppet bodies in this world. And I see, standing with them, others their equal. In that moment, everything I had ever been scared of becomes, by comparison, inconsequential.

Cara and I scramble back as a massive black clawed hand grabs the void's black edges and starts tearing it further open.

"Oh sister, what have you done?" Claire gasps.

A dark shape, eyes burning red, crawls through the tear between our worlds, small and crablike with four legs, each ending in a single sharp claw. It leaps to a chandelier and then onto the face of a soldier in the front row. The creature dissolves into the soldier's head. The soldier's expression shifts dramatically, through fear to pain and finally to a blank stare. He calmly slides his langseax out of its sheath and buries it into the forehead of the soldier beside him.

"Time to leave," Allison says rather urgently as she pulls on my arm.

Another dark shape, the entity that had been tearing open the veil, steps through the tear between our worlds. Its distorted humanoid shape, with perversely-shaped limbs that bend inhumanly at the knees and oversized arms, stalks towards the nearest person, the Marshal. The entity gives him no chance. It swings its massive arms, claws connecting with the Marshal's head. With an audible snap, his neck bends at an impossible angle. The creature tears the Marshal's head off and throws the body, twisted and broken, in front of the podium. The room explodes into chaos.

"This way!" Erik yells at us. "There's got to be another door at the back."

Claire scrambles to grab the cage containing Macha. With her and Cara beside me, and with Caitlin already following Allison, we all run toward Erik. The soldiers are so focused on the entities stepping through the veil that none of them pay any attention to us as we scramble to find an exit.

The first door we come across, an old wooden door, is locked. Erik holds his hand toward it, palm forward, expecting to be able to break it down telekinetically, forgetting the bracelets we all wear. When that doesn't work, Allison shoulders the door, trying to bust through it. Still the solid door doesn't budge. And we're starting to get noticed.

I gently hold Allison back with one hand while reaching over her shoulder with the other. In my mind I picture the door blowing outward. The process seems simple now. The force travels down my arm and out my hand, a black tendril spiralling towards the door. It cracks into a dozen pieces, each traveling their own paths for metres down the hallway on the other side.

"What about the others?" Claire asks.

Erik shakes his head. "There's no going back for them."

As we run down a hall way, the screams quiet down, replaced with the sickening sounds of flesh and bones being torn apart.

"Where the hell are we?" Caitlin says.

"I don't care, just try to find a way out," Erik replies.

We end up in a small room. Judging by the uniforms draped over a desk in the centre, it must have belonged to the Marshal. The wall to the left of the door we came in is dedicated to an elaborate bookcase filled floor to ceiling with ancient books. The massive wooden desk in the centre is ancient; a well-used wooden armchair sits behind it. The wall behind those, to our right is filled from one side to the other with ancient wooden drawers, with more Templar banners hanging from the ceiling above them.

"It's beautiful," Cara says, running her fingertips over the desk.

"Grab anything useful you see. Try to find something that will get these bracelets off," Erik suggests.

Allison climbs onto the armchair and looks at a glass display cabinet that's attached to the wall above the drawers. Failing to find a way to open it, she smashes the glass with her elbow and pulls out two long swords, held in plain leather scabbards wrapped with material of white and red.

She jumps down off the chair and carefully draws one of the swords; its dark-steel blade a metre long from point to cruciform hilt.

"Do you trust me?" Allison says with a grin, pointing the sword at Erik's bracelet.

Erik just raises an eyebrow at her. Allison shrugs, slides the sword back in its scabbard and slips it across her back.

"I could try cutting them off with telekinesis," I offer.

Erik gestures down the hallway we just came through, littered with the shattered pieces of door. "Not a fucking chance."

Noises echo from the hall.

"Nevermind!" Erik says.

Allison throws him the other sword. The door out of this room is unlocked, thankfully. We burst out of the room, into the pouring rain but still within the massive concrete walls of the fortress. Erik motions to us to be silent, and points off into the distance, at a large passageway set into the castle wall. The main thoroughfare into the keep. A patrol of soldiers mill around nearby, unloading a small convoy of military trucks waiting just inside the passageway.

Then the main doors of the temple burst open. Cara flinches, swearing to herself. Soldiers come stumbling out, some screaming and yelling, others... quieter. One soldier trips, falling backwards. The black creatures are quickly upon him, one latching onto his head. He twitches once and then lies still. An enormous black humanoid, a giant by human standards with massive black tendrils held up from his back like wings, walks over to the soldier's body and picks it off the ground. The entity shakes the lifeless body and then places it back in its feet. The soldier opens his eyes, deep red burning brightly. Then, with weapon raised, he charges off towards the trucks at the main gate. The possessed pounces on the first soldier he comes upon, stabbing him through the chest with his langseax. The retaliation from the other soldiers at the main gate is swift. They cut the possessed soldier to pieces. As each blow from their knives connect, wisps of black tendrils flare out from the soldier before they fade away. For a brief moment the massive entity looks in our direction, then turns away, letting out a wicked laugh.

Alarms ring out along the ramparts. Activity explodes around the fortress. Across the courtyard, other soldiers pour from of a long building while the soldiers near the main gate slowly edge their way towards them.

More red-eyed soldiers pour from the temple, most of whom, judging by their wounds, shouldn't be alive. None appear to be truly living. The two groups stand across the courtyard from each other, the living versus the possessed, with us hiding in shadows but very much in the middle of it all. I'm not sure what the soldiers at the gate believe they can do against the gathering possessed.

"How are we going to get past all this?" I whisper.

An order is shouted out from the living side, audible over the howling of the possessed, as soldiers form battle lines next to their barracks and cut off the main gate. Neither group moves. Dark entities stalk outside the temple, taunting and howling at the soldiers at the main gate. The entities appear to be toying with the living. I watch as three dog like entities, as large as wolves, stalk unnoticed around the side of the courtyard and wait in the shadows, only their glowing red eyes giving away their presence. Not all the entities leaving the temple join the growing entity army. Some crawl up the walls of the fortress and disappear over the edge. Out into the night.

"I have an idea," Claire whispers before hesitating. I follow her gaze. A small group of men, including the guard who brought me food, march rapidly towards the living army, their path leading them near the hidden wolf entities. As their path crosses directly in front of the wolf creatures, the group of soldiers hesitate for a moment. They all stop and shake their heads, looking around as if confused. Then, recovering quickly, they continue safely passed the hidden wolf entities, towards the rest of the living. Claire lets out her breath. I breathe my own sigh of relief.

"If we move slowly, I can cloak our presence from the minds of the soldiers," Claire whispers. "Though I'm not sure about those creatures."

"How are you able to do that wearing..." my sentence trails off when I realise she isn't wearing bracelets. "How come you're not wearing any of these?"

"Long story short, they only a have a few. With all you here, there wasn't enough, so they took some off us. Sometimes, the threat of having a bullet placed into your brain is often the best deterrent. Now's not the time to explain. You all need to stay close to me. And this is only going to work for a short distance. So once we're past the trucks, get ready to run."

It's a tense walk as move in plain sight towards the living soldiers. There are moments, when I'm certain the soldiers are looking me directly in the eyes. Yet none of them raise any alert. Perhaps they're too focused on the dark creatures and possessed soldiers across the courtyard. We slowly weave through the trucks, trying to avoid any sudden moment. I can't believe we've made it this far with none of them noticing. Claire stops us just outside the castle. We huddled close.

"This is as far as I can get us, with this rain as it is," she whispers. "They'll start to be able to see us the further away we move."

"Where are we going from here?" Caitlin asks.

"Head to the trees," Allison whispers, pointing towards a line of pines about a hundred metres in the distance. "Get ready..."

Then all hell breaks loose behind us.

"Run for it," Erik says, dropping any pretence of stealth.

Our presence is quickly noticed.

"Stop them!" Soldiers shout in alarm on the ramparts above us.

"This way!" Erik yells.

The first gunshots ring out as we're halfway across the field to the trees. Close. Really close.

"Erik, Duck!" Cara yells.

Another volley. Erik flinches as a bullet whizzes past his head. Cara cries out as a bullet wings her, red slicing across her right arm. I stop to help her.

"Don't stop, keep going!" Erik yells back at us.

I grab Cara's hand as we run. We're at the tree-line before I realise the shooting had stopped well before we made it. Hiding ourselves behind the tree line, we take a moment to recover and look back at the castle. And watch in horror as veil creatures appear on the walls and overwhelm the guards on the ramparts. Allison grabs Erik's shoulder and points towards the gateway.

"What the hell is happening?" Allison asks.

A hellish scream carries over the field. An army of Templars, their aberrant red eyes cutting through the misty rain, swarm out of the entrance and start running at an unnatural speed towards us. Dark entities surround them as the army charges across the field; proverbial hellhounds of different shapes bound on either side while giant humanoid entities take up the rear and winged creatures of many shapes fly overhead. The first supernatural howls flood over the fields.

"Run!" Erik yells as we take off through the trees. "Stay together!"

We turn and bolt, aiming blindly through the trees. Branches cut painfully. The further in we run, the more we struggle to stay together in the thickening wood. I slip and stumble, losing one of these terrible shoes. Cara is there to lift me back up. With no time to find the lost shoe, I throw the other away. My feet quickly go numb from the pain of running barefoot through the rough undergrowth. Still we run. Glowing eyes materialise in the darkness, close behind us. Howls pierce the air. Close.

"Keep going!" Erik yells from somewhere up ahead.

I can see the first entities close behind us now. Too close. Then the first of the soldiers, they're catching up. The hellhounds race up until they're flanking us, perhaps 20 metres on both sides, and start closing in.

There! A break in the trees.

It Wasn't Supposed To End like This

The Viridis River flowing in front of me kills any further hope of escape. While the river appears shallow enough to cross, the water is waist high and there's no clear path across. Thousands of floating pine needles fill the flowing river, washed there by the freezing rain that soaks through me. We huddle together, shivering, on the bank of the river, waiting for our pursuers to appear.

Slowly, the first Templar stalks out of the trees, his glowing red eyes and shadowy haze showing that he's no longer entirely human. Dark shapes, hell-hounds and other sinister entities slink out of the woods. They pace along the shore, watching us, waiting. Behind me, Erik and Allison draw their swords and stand ready. Another Templar arrives, then another. Soon there is a flood of them, all holding their wicked knives out at the ready. They slowly edge forward. There's no urgency in their movement; the hunt is over.

It wasn't supposed to end like this. To get so far, to find my sister, to do the impossible and get her out of there, only to end up in this dead-end situation.

Together, we edge backwards, into the freezing river, hopelessly putting off the inevitable.

Enough of this! Fury builds within me, at myself, for causing this. Haven't I caused enough pain to everyone already? Why the fuck should these people suffer because of who I am? Why did Aine have to die because of who I am? I promised Claire that today would be ok. Nothing is going to cause any more pain to these people. Not today. I have no idea what I'm going to do. But what does it matter? In this moment I'm willing to give everything just to save the people behind me.

I scream; raw unbridled fury, "If you want me, come and take me!"

I start wading back to river bank. Towards the swarm. There is a purity to my fury; this newfound hyperawareness of my potential with any pretence of hesitation gone. Time slows for me, each movement, each breath of all the frenzied soldiers played out in slow motion before me. I lash out with all the force I can generate at the Templar nearest me. Black splits the air between us. He falls forward, dead, but I've already moved on to the next. Again and again I lash out. It becomes so automatic I take the time to reach down and collect a fallen langseax; total emotional detachment. Lightning flashes. Around me, I see their every moment before they make it. Many futures layered across the world around me. Still they swarm in. I bury the knife deep one soldier's head while more black tendrils pierce the bodies around me. I swing the knife freely, hacking away. It's a poor tool for the job, but at least it bites again and again. It hardly matters as long as crimson flows. I swing again and again and again. Crimson waves lap against the shore.

Something grabs me by the shoulder. I swing the knife, ready to fight back. Allison grabs my wrist moments before I embed it in her head.

"Stop! They're all dead. Look, they others, aren't coming closer. Come on, we need to get across this river before they change their minds."

Wicked laughter rolls across the river from deep within the pine woods. I look up at her in a daze, hands dripping in blood. Frightened of what I almost did. Then a wave of exhaustion crashes over me and I collapse into the cold water; the price extracted for all my efforts.

"Erik! Help me carry her..." her voice slowly fades out as the world turns black.

♦

I don't remember much of what happens next. Only the constant shivering as Erik carries me and the fact my nose just won't stop leaking. I try apologising.

"Shhh," Cara whispers from somewhere unseen.

I pass out again.

Just the Beginning

I open my eyes to find Cara's face close in front of mine as she kneels next to me. An indigo twilight sky hangs over the trees above me as the massive tree trunk I'm propped against digs roughly into my back. I'm soaking wet, but at least the rain has stopped.

Her face lights up. "I knew you'd be awake soon," she says, happily. "It's good to see you're ok."

She hands a soldier's langseax to me, handle first. "This clearly belongs to you now."

I nod. The smooth grip fits comfortably into my hand. I place it next to me

"Where are we?"

"We're still in the woods, on the outer side of the river. The others are talking about how to get out of here, because at the moment we're thoroughly lost. Our sisters are currently arguing about the best method for finding out where we are," she laughs.

"And the Templars?" I ask.

"There's been nothing since the river, thankfully. But..."

She shrugs as she sits down to the left of me, leaning against the tree. She flinches as her arm brushes against mine. Her sleeve is covered in blood. Dried blood covers the back of her hand where it's run down her arm.

"Are you going to be ok?" I ask.

"I'll survive," she says. "Still, it fucking hurts."

I notice though, looking closer under the tear in her sleeve, that the blood on her arm is still bright red.

"Shit, you're still bleeding. You can't leave it like that. Here."

With a gentle hand to hold her arm steady, I take the long knife and cut the sleeve off above her cut. She flinches again, biting her lip in pain, as my fingers get too close. The cut is deep.

"It'll leave a nice scar. At least it's clean through."

Taking off my own shirt, I hack away at it, cutting off a rough strip from the bottom. Cara watches what I do closely; smiling at me despite the pain she knows is coming. She winces as I wrap the strip around her arm. Closes her eyes and moans as I tie it off. A breath released in relief.

"How does that feel?"

She nods and smiles graciously at me. "Thank you."

Her eyes remain locked with me, staring deeply into me. She's beautiful and right there I want nothing more than to kiss her. Thank her for everything she's done for me.

She leans forward. Before I realise what she's doing, soft lips close against mine, for just a moment. Bewitching eyes watch my reaction. A shared breath as her lips hover a fraction off mine. A flirtatious grin as she pulls away.

"I didn't need clairvoyance to tell what you were thinking," she whispers.

I fall back into my makeshift seat, ecstatic. Her hand finds mine. A delicate squeeze.

"There plenty more of that to be had later," she says.

"Later indeed," Nem says, out of nowhere. Looking up, I see her sitting next her sister on a branch hanging above us, their legs swinging playfully.

"How?" I ask, surprised.

"What? No apology for tearing me apart?" Nem says with mock indignation. "You didn't think you'd actually killed me? It'd take a little more than that. And by 'little', I mean it's less than possible; certainly in the traditional sense anyway. And while I am glad that you've finally tapped into all that newfound power, I really do wish you'd let me help you achieve it in a more controlled way. As you have now found out, there is some serious fallout for reaching into the veil in an uncontrolled manner like you did. And what the fuck were you doing trusting Lucian's advice? Silly girl."

"What, was I just supposed to let her die? I couldn't lose her. I couldn't."

"While I can see how important she is to you the price you paid for her life today could well be paid with the lives of everyone later."

They both pause and look around suddenly.

"Still, that's something you'll have to work out later. Tonight, I suggest you get as far away from here as possible. Treasure this shared moment, as you may not get another chance to. The fallout from your decision will land at your feet, soon enough. Be ready."

Cara leans towards me. "I, at least, am thankful for what you did," she whispers into my ear. Then she presses her lips again to the corner of mine, a gentle loving kiss. She doesn't pull away.

"Ah, sorry to interrupt..." Claire walks over to us at the most inopportune time. "I'm glad at least to see you're awake and ok, sister," she says. "I guess we can talk a lot more later. We've obviously got a lot of catching up to do. But there's something that I need to know. It can't wait. What happened to Sophie?"

"Sophie?" I ask, confused.

"You don't remember our little sister Sophie?"

"I don't..." my voice trails off as something deep within me shatters, and memories come flooding back. And I saw what a foolish girl I'd been.

I do remember. The wrapped up bundle in Mum's arms when they found me. The little girl I was supposed to keep safe under the bed. Baby Sophie had been upset all day and Mum and Dad were both so focused on her. I was supposed to be the big grown up sister and play by myself. But I didn't want to; I wanted them to play with me. I was jealous. Why wouldn't they play with me? So I ran away. I wanted them to know how much they'd miss me.

And because I ran away, they didn't notice the warning signs of the raid until it was too late. And I remember the three crows sitting on the tree above me, guarding over my hiding spot. Leading Claire to me.

"I'm starting to remember now." I say, staring off into the distance. I struggle to keep myself composed. This is entirely my fault.

"You were there that day," I say to Nem and Macha.

"Of course," they both respond.

"Why did you let Claire get captured that day?"

"Because there were entities there that day that were beyond even our ability to handle," Macha says. "To keep you all safe, we have had to play the long game."

The long game... That phrase triggers more memories; memories of things that occurred after that day. I know why I couldn't remember Sophie.

"In the years after the raid, the government were constantly looking for us. They knew we existed. I hid for so long. But they were always getting closer. And the older I got, the more I realised what mattered the most to me. Sophie had a family that cared for her. She was safe. I was the weak link. Constantly on the run. Always too close to being captured.

"Even before, as children, Claire and I were capable of so many talented things. Our parents taught us everything. We didn't have to wait to grow into our talents like others do. I never was a late bloomer with my own talents. It was all a lie.

"I remember the day I realised I couldn't risk it anymore. I was twelve." More memories come flooding back to me, hazy after all these years, but slowly coming back to me.

"The first construct was to tear the memory of Sophie from the minds of all those who had come in contact with her and me together and then lock those same memories away from my own reach so that I could never giver her up. The second construct was to lock my own memories of Claire away. It was to invent a childhood of memories and wait patiently over the years for the right time to shatter that lock and find her again. The final construct was a phoenix, a store of energy and memories that, as a dead-man's switch, was ready to trigger if I ever got so close to danger that only my talents could save me. Its final purpose was to lock away my own talents so that I would never stand out and become an obvious target for the government. It was... to hold what it meant to be me, a reflection of all of who I was before that faithful day."

"Hmmm, your memory still needs some work," Nem says from above, and then jumps down to stand, in human form, before me.

"But we forgive you anyway, for referring to us as mindless constructs," Macha says, joining her on the ground.

"Like I've told you before, we aren't just constructs. We are much more than that," Nem says. "We, as entities, have existed for thousands of years, watching over warriors that fight for this world, aiding them in the eternal battles to keep the veil out of this world."

"We were always there, watching over you and your sisters, just like we've watched over many warriors before you." Macha continues. "But you knew we couldn't keep you safe forever. We hatched this plan together to keep you all safe."

"Why not just tell me?"

"Because we couldn't. That was part of the promise. For the plan to work, we too had to be part of the process. It was important that we played our parts in the grand play perfectly. As things unfold, more is unlocked for us."

"And this is only the first move," Nem adds. "The next one will come soon enough. You need to get away from this area and out of these woods. They're coming for you..."

Claire reaches out and offers me a hand up.

"Thank you, dear sister. You've sacrificed so much to protect our baby sister. We need to find her. This is just the beginning of our story together, my little Eve."

About the Author

Ben Wise was born in Sydney Australia though quickly abandoned the place for sunnier Queensland. He studied Software Engineering and Crimson started as an escape from the insanity of his job as a 29 year old programmer/solution architect. Work suffered as he enjoyed the many late nights narrating Eve's story far too much. Crimson is his first book.

www.ingramcontent.com/pod-product-compliance
Lightning Source LLC
Chambersburg PA
CBHW060153130626
46556CB00006B/2620